Down the Plymouth Road

An Indirect Spiritual Autobiography

by Stanley Jenkins

A THURSTON HOWL PUBLICATIONS BOOK

ISBN 978-1-945247-38-5

DOWN THE PLYMOUTH ROAD

Copyright © 2018 by Stanley Jenkins

Edited by Thurston Howl
Book design by Thurston Howl
Cover design by Thurston Howl
Cover art by Tabsley © 2018

First edition, 2018. All rights reserved.

A Thurston Howl Publications Book
Published by Thurston Howl Publications
thurstonhowlpublications.com
Lansing, MI

For Mary.

"...work out your own salvation with fear and trembling..."
Philippians 2:12, NRSV

Itinerary

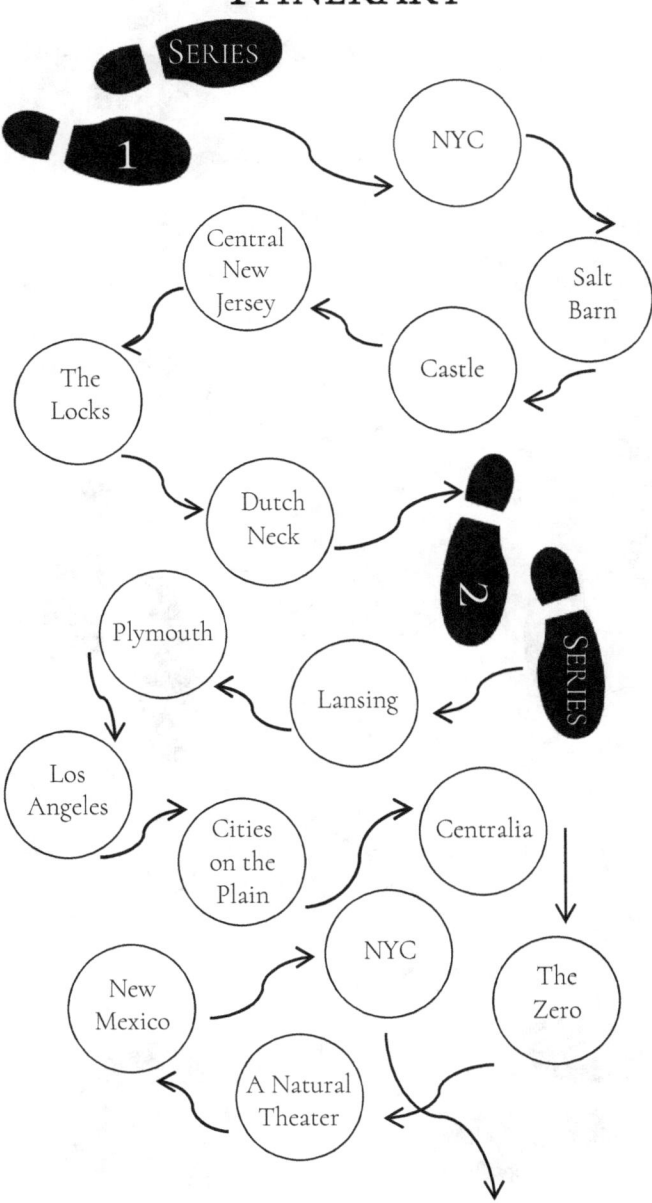

Series 1 → NYC → Salt Barn → Castle → Central New Jersey → The Locks → Dutch Neck → Series 2 → Lansing → Plymouth → Los Angeles → Cities on the Plain → Centralia → The Zero → New Mexico → NYC → A Natural Theater

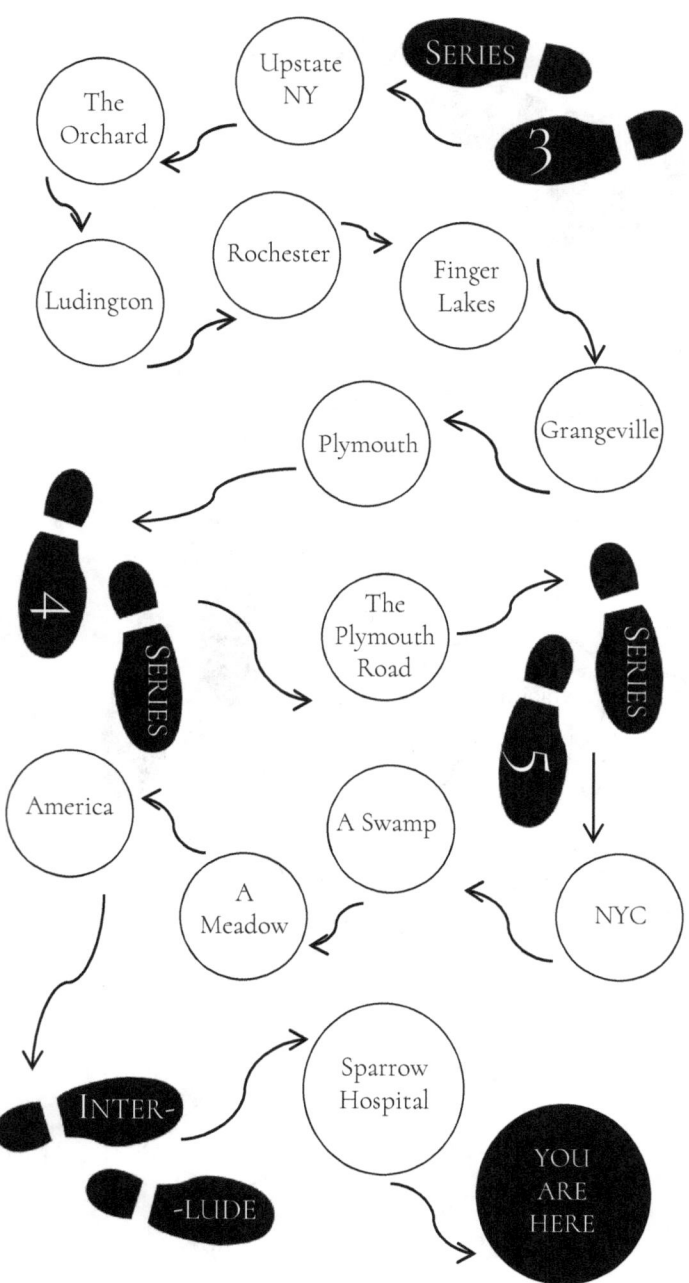

Introduction

In October of this year (2018), I will celebrate the 30th anniversary of my Ordination as a Minister of the Word and Sacrament in the Presbyterian Church (USA). Please don't let that scare you.

I have no intention of proselytizing to you, judging you, or promulgating the ugly, authoritarian toxin coming forth from so many mouths of those who claim authority to speak in the name of Jesus Christ or the GOP and see no daylight between the two. We've had enough of that.

But I do want to claim your attention. Whether you are religious, spiritual, or not. I want to move you. Irritate you. Make you laugh. I want to keep company with you.

But in order to do that, I have to be honest. Or at least as honest as I am capable of being. So in this book, this collection of parables, prose poems, memoirs, skits, and skreeds, I'm speaking to you in the language I know, the language of fable and scripture, ritual and repetition. The overflowing excess of love and intimacy—and the ego's fear of being drowned, swallowed. I'm speaking to you in the language of sin. *Midrash.* Violence. History. Corny jokes. The language of one who has always arrived but has to keep walking.

Listen. Look. There is the Plymouth Road. It comes first. It is a two-way mirror. And you are on both sides of it. It is a stage for images. There are voices, and you just know that they are the voices of actors you can't see. Kafka's "Nature Theatre of Oklahoma," Hesse's "Magic Theater." Times Square in the mid-eighties. They are performing strange Passion Plays.

And then there is the Rabbi. He's slightly sinister. *Who knows what evil lurks in the hearts of men? The Shadow knows.* He's shabby, his face shrouded in a moth-eaten black hat, until it isn't, and then he is radiant. And when he is radiant.... And the next thing you know, you are passing a bottle back and forth. But this is a new kind of intoxication.

Then, there is Pilgrim, and Pilgrim is "you" in the same way that Rimbaud's "I" is "another." He is stubborn and mulish and then suddenly earnest and joyful. He is along for the ride and engineering every inch of the road. He wears a cardigan sweater and looks as if he might ask you for money.

And now enter the Devil. He has the eyes you are always avoiding. He owns your shame and can't be trusted. His face is bloated, and he requires that you reflect a lie back to him. You are his mirror.

They are all walking down the Plymouth Road. Just waiting for you.

SERIES ONE

"Jesus said, 'Become passers-by.'"
The Gospel of Thomas

1

I was walking down the Plymouth Road with the Rabbi, and he was showing me stuff.

He showed me this homeless guy who lived at the 79th St. Boat Basin. He'd been a boxer. He was a loser. He died of exposure one cold night.

He showed me this old lady living in a luxury apartment on Grand Ave. in Queens. Her husband died. And then her brother died. And then she started to sell her possessions and her fancy clothes. And they evicted her, and she went into the shelter system and was just swallowed.

He showed me this woman who had a cyst on her ovary and told this guy she knew that she was going to die and tried to get the guy to adopt her son. And the cyst was benign, and she'd been trying to pawn the kid off on anyone she could find. She was done being a mother. The kid set the apartment on fire and died in the flames.

I was walking with the Rabbi, and he was showing me stuff.

"Why you got to show me this stuff?" I asked.

He lifted his arm, and with the rustling of the cape, I caught a whiff of a city-run old folks' home.

"We're chasing daylight here," he said. "We don't have a lot of time."

"No, seriously. Why do I have to see all this stuff? What about the other stuff?"

"The other stuff? Son, you don't know what you're asking."

"Oh, come on!"

He lifted his other arm, and, with the rustling of the cape, I caught a glimpse of the hyena and the gazelle.

"Son, you're not ready."

"But...."

He lifted his eyes, and what I saw in the twinkling of an eye....

I was not ready.

I was walking to Plymouth, and I met the Rabbi on the road. He was laughing.

"What are you laughing about?" I asked.

"Check this out," he said and then held up an iPad. "It's a slideshow of all your former selves."

I took a look and winced.

"C'mon, you were so cute!"

"You're sick, you know that?" but I was kind of laughing myself. I lingered over one of the former selves. "What was I thinking?"

"I know, right?"

"Well," I asked, "are we going to do this thing?"

"Might as well get started."

He pulled out the straight razor and removed my skin. I stood there without my skin.

"It's still not deep enough, is it?" I asked.

"No, it's not."

"Rabbi, can I have my eyebrows back? The sun is so bright, and I need to squint."

He gave me my eyebrows back. I squinted. I felt the wind on my muscles, so raw now without skin.

I walked down the Plymouth Road.

I was walking down the Plymouth Road, and I came upon the Devil. He broke my jaw. Just hauled off and busted me in the chops.

"What you want to go and do a thing like that for?" I asked, all blood and outrage.

"You got a big mouth, Pilgrim," he said. "I hear you been talking."

"I didn't give nothing away," I pleaded

He broke my nose.

"Listen bitch, I decide what it means to give something away! You got that?"

"I didn't say nothing! You didn't have to go and do that!"

"You make me sick," he said. "You couldn't keep a secret if your life depended on it. You're weak. You're a joke. You're *nothing*!"

"And...scene."

We both cracked up.

"Jeeze, you didn't have to really break my nose," I cried.

"What about you? 'I must pay the rent! I can't pay the rent!' You're such a diva!"

We sort of collapsed together in hilarity, me and the Devil.

After a while, it kind of hurts your stomach to keep laughing.

"You do know that you can break every bone in my body, and I will still find my way home, right?"

"Yeah, I know."

"Then, why do you keep ambushing me on the road?"

"It ain't personal, kid; it's just business."

"Anyway, I just want you to know I don't hold a grudge."

"Well, that's just fine."

"That's the way the cookie crumbles."

"You're alright, Pilgrim."

"You're not so bad yourself."

I stuck him with my knife like a pig.

There is a room where they keep all the sorrow. It looks a lot like a salt barn in the northeast. In any case, it's very easy to get a pass to enter that room. To enter the room of sorrow.

There is another room where they keep all the ecstasy. It looks a lot like a salt barn in the northeast. And you can wait your whole life and never get a pass to enter the room of ecstasy.

You go down the road long enough, and you realize that it's the same room. The room where they keep all the sorrow and the room where they keep all the ecstasy. It looks a lot like a salt barn in the northeast.

I've been down the road long enough, and I don't really know what to make of that. It's the same room. It's the same frigging room.

It was either the Rabbi or the Devil who told me once that I was the salt of the earth. Truth be told, sometimes they sound a lot alike. And if you *really* want to know the truth, sometimes I have a hard time telling them apart.

None of that really matters though. They give you a pass to enter the room when you're born. It looks a lot like a salt barn in the northeast.

What you do with the pass is up to you.

I was further on down the road, and I met the Rabbi. He was waiting for me and said, "I got something you need to see." And he showed me his iPad, and there was just nothing on that screen.

"I know what you did," he said.

"I don't even know how to begin to feel guilty," I said.

"I'm not asking you to feel guilty."

"Then, what's your point?"

"Once there was a seed," he said, "and it grew large and became a tree and many birds made their homes in its branches."

"And that tree killed the lawn and was a bit of an eyesore in the neighborhood. What's your point?"

"Yeah, but the birds...they had a place to build their nests."

"So what? The world is full of opportunists."

"Don't give me that; you know what it means to have others depend on you."

"Once," I said, "I dreamed that all the trees walked about when we were asleep. It was a lie, wasn't it?"

"I'm afraid so, Pilgrim."

"Still, it hurts to set roots...."

"....because they will always be pulled up."

"Yep."

"And birds will always need somewhere to nest," he said.

"Rabbi?"

"Yes?"

"The birds...You sent them, didn't you?"

"I sent the birds."

"Rabbi?"

"Yes?"

"Thank you."

"You're welcome. Now, hand over that knife: there's been enough killing for the day."

I was walking down the Plymouth Road, my feet like roots newly ripped from fertile soil, flinging dirt across the road.

They got the whole deal set up on the Plymouth Road. It's like a spiritual toll system. You want to get from point A to point B? You got to pay the man.

At regular intervals, you encounter fearsome angels with fiery swords. If you do not have the secret password—the secret name of the angel—why, that angel is just going to cut you down. You will drown on the steps of marble; you will emerge from the orchard a broken man. And worst of all, you will not make your connecting flight.

Because, after all, it is all about getting home for the holidays.

On the Plymouth Road, everywhere you look now, they got fiery chariots ascending and descending. They got prophets on their way up and they got prophets on their way down. Ascending and descending in fiery chariots. This is all on the Plymouth Road, you understand.

And sometimes, the way forward flows from the cracked lips of the prophet on his way up, and other times it flows from the bleeding lips of the prophet who is on his way down. Either way, you've got to maintain your sea legs when the way forward flows.

Yes, indeedy! They got it all worked out on the Plymouth Road. It's where the weight of your life finds the foundation to hold it! Woo doggie!

Listen up, folks! They're going to try and tell you that you're doomed. I mean, on the Plymouth Road. All the demons snapping at your heels. All those demons—they are just forever waiting to tell you that you are doomed. But they're wrong.

You're not doomed. You're just not home yet—gotta ways to go yet, that's all—on the Plymouth Road.

Might as well splurge on a brand-new pair of shoes when you know you're going to need them. Know what I mean?

I was walking down the Plymouth Road, and the Rabbi was walking too.

"I guess we're pretty much stuck with one another," I said.

"I guess," he replied.

"Rabbi?"

"Yes?"

And then after a while, I said, "Never mind."

We just walked down the Plymouth Road.

2

I was walking down the Plymouth Road; it was just me and the Rabbi, and then we came upon Jesus. He was hiding ridiculously behind a potted plant. Invisible in plain sight like a purloined letter. We waved at him and called his name, but he just ignored us.

"You know we can see you," I said.

I turned to the Rabbi, but he was nowhere to be found.

"You're not fooling anyone behind that potted plant," I said. "In fact, the whole thing is really kind of infantile. We can see you. I'm just saying."

"Maybe he doesn't want to be seen," the Rabbi said. "Maybe you should just ignore him."

I turned to say something, but the Rabbi was nowhere to be found. Jesus peered out from behind the potted plant.

"But I can see you!" I shouted.

"There's no need to get worked up about it," the Rabbi said.

I was starting to get angry. This was just stupid.

"I mean...you're right there!"

"You really need to learn to let it go, Pilgrim."

We just kept walking, me and the Rabbi.

"It just chaps my ass...."

"I'm just saying...let it go."

"He was right *there*."

I got a castle in my soul, and you can't enter into this castle unless you take off your shoes. God lives in the castle in my soul—but when God enters, even the Father, Son, and Holy Ghost wait outside. (This is true up to the point at which it becomes a lie. It's not like I'm some kind of Unitarian, or something.)

I got a castle in my soul, and it only becomes manifest when I build it. My ancestors used to sing a song: "Working on a building, a Holy Ghost building!"

This is what they were talking about. There is always something else that we are doing whenever we do what we are doing. I suspect that what the ancestors referred to as "Wisdom" was the ability to see double.

I got a castle in my soul, and the bride and the bridegroom, they enter therein. They close the doors; they draw up the bridge. What goes on between them in the castle in my soul is not for my eyes. But I'd be a fool not to join the party outside the castle walls. I'd be a fool not to dance to such music.

I got a castle in my soul. I've spent half my life besieging it and the other half trying to tear it down from within. It just always stands. It doesn't feel my assaults. It just always stands.

I got a castle in my soul, and the banners that fly from its spires and minarets are spectacular. They just really are something else.

I was walking down the Plymouth Road, and the Rabbi turned to me and said, "You thought it would be different, didn't you?"

"I guess I did."

"You thought maybe by shedding all that skin and cutting all those roots, you'd feel free."

"But all I feel is rootless."

"You thought that you could just throw away everything you didn't need."

"And all I feel is vulnerable."

"It gets better."

"I know. But I'm not as strong as you."

He laughed. "I'm not as strong as me, either."

That cracked me up.

"We walk," he said, "and it's not personal."

"But it's always personal," I said.

"Why can't it be both?" he said.

"When I was young, I knew joy, and it was something other than where I came from."

"And then you got older and found out there was no joy worth having if it didn't include where you came from."

"Rabbi?"

"Yes?"

"I would miss you if you were gone."

"I'm never here."

"But I'm not alone."

"Just keep walking, Pilgrim. Just keep walking."

"I can feel the joy of the man I'm going to become."

"Just keep walking. Just keep walking."

3

I was walking down the Plymouth Road, and the Rabbi was there too. And I came upon a man who was carrying a load he couldn't bear or cast off. It seemed alive and changed shape with every step, as it undulated and heaved in his arms like the sea.

I thought I saw weasels, wolverines, and badgers, vicious in panic, musky in distress, dart from the load and bite the man's cheek. I thought I saw warm kisses and soft lips, a sigh and a relenting.

My heart was full of pity, and I wept for my brother.

"Why do you weep?" the Rabbi asked.

"Because my brother loves what he hates and hates what he loves."

"So, why is *your* face is bleeding?" the Rabbi asked.

"My face is bleeding because these tears turn to glass, and they are sharp."

"The weasels, the wolverines, and the badgers—they are eating your face, aren't they?"

I cracked up. I couldn't help it: it was the way he said it.

"Yeah."

"And this is what you've lived your whole life longing for, isn't it?"

I nodded.

"Didn't I tell you to maintain your boundaries?"

He asked this so tenderly. I choked up and fell into his arms, right there on the Plymouth Road, where they sell your eyes for a quarter and no man is ever sure of his companion.

"Trust me on this one, Pilgrim," he whispered, as I rested in his arms, "you can always find a face when you need one."

My ears bled at the touch of his breath on my neck.

"Thank you," I said.

"Don't mention it."

I carried my load down the Plymouth Road, and the Rabbi was with me. We were smiling, and, for an instant, it seemed as if we were both invisible.

And it was good.

We just walked a while, me, the Rabbi, and my brother, down the Plymouth Road, carrying our loads. And it was good.

I was walking down the Plymouth Road, and the Rabbi was there too. And I saw my brother, but my brother was no different from me. He walked beside me, and he walked in lock-step, and he really kind of freaked me out. When I went up, he went up, and when I went down, he went down. Lock-step.

The first thing I thought when I saw my brother was that I didn't want to be tied down like that. You go up, you go down. But when you are up and they go down, it just really inhibits your mobility. The first thing they teach you in life-saving is how to break someone's arm, so the drowner doesn't, in a panic, take you down with them.

"What kind of stunt are you pulling here?" I asked the Rabbi.

"Get used to it, kid," he said. "You're going to need to walk blind, and, when you do, you're going to need your brother."

"But..."

"Don't be a fool, it's not like he trusts you either."

"I mean..."

"Don't even try: it's all about the rhythm, and you've always known that."

"Doesn't mean I've always known how to keep the beat."

"Your brother is here. Why don't you just walk with him?"

"Like I have a choice!"

"Don't be petulant."

My brother sort of looked at me out the corner of his eye. I acknowledged his presence. He was kind of shy. We just walked a while, me, my brother, and the Rabbi. I was intrigued.

Still, I was pissed, didn't want to meet the Rabbi's eye...

We just kept walking. Me and my brother and the Rabbi.

I was walking down the Plymouth Road with my brother and the Rabbi, and I kept seeing artichoke hearts. All along the road, there were artichoke hearts.

"Someone's had their leaves shorn," I said, "am I right?"

I looked at my brother and the Rabbi for some you-got-that-right-kid, but they just looked at me. There was an uncomfortable silence.

"I'm just saying, someone's going to have a rude awakening; someone's going to have to look in the mirror."

My brother and the Rabbi looked embarrassed.

"I'm not wearing any pants, am I?"

We just walked.

"Son of a bitch!"

"It's alright, Pilgrim," the Rabbi said, "happens to the best of us."

"You want me to take *my* pants off?" my brother asked, swallowing a laugh.

"I don't even like artichoke hearts," I said.

My brother and the Rabbi burst out laughing.

I was so pissed, but I was laughing too.

"What the hell?" I cried in mock outrage.

We laughed so hard my sides like to burst, artichoke hearts everywhere you looked.

The Devil Berates Pilgrim
and Pilgrim Seduces the Devil

THE DEVIL: You just keep flapping your gums. You just keep writing checks, but you got nothing in the bank.

PILGRIM: It all depends on what you mean by nothing.

THE DEVIL: It's winners and losers in this world, and there's no neutral ground.

PILGRIM: I've seen that movie, and neither of us were in it.

THE DEVIL: You'll see, everyone pays in the end.

PILGRIM: I bought the ticket; I'll take the ride.

THE DEVIL: You'll be sorry.

PILGRIM: Among other things.
            (*Pilgrim pauses.*)

PILGRIM: Have you lost weight? You look good.

THE DEVIL: Well, I have been eating my vegetables.

PILGRIM: Whatever you're doing, keep doing it.

THE DEVIL: I know what you're doing.

PILGRIM: I know, but we both know we can't resist it.

THE DEVIL: You're little, and I will devour you.

PILGRIM: I bet you could. You're so strong.

THE DEVIL: I hate you.

PILGRIM: Did you know you're eyes are beautiful when you're mad?

Mr. Bournesmith

When Mr. Bournesmith finally arrived, his limousine having been detained on Route 1, he entered a local high school gymnasium in Central New Jersey and opened his mouth. There was a pep rally going on at the time, so the kids were pretty much savages to begin with. Loaded for bear. Whipped up. I mean, you just knew someone was going to have to pay.

He opened his mouth.

But before that, he grew, he just kept getting bigger, and he was pretty big to begin with. It was becoming alarming. His body had always been plump and not just fat, but plump, like you wanted to get close, like there was ripeness and safety, if you could just burrow in, snuggle up—cling to his girth. But he just kept growing until his girth smothered everything around it.

When Mr. Bournesmith finally arrived, bleachers were bulldozed out of alignment as his belly advanced. There was a horrible sound of metal stretching as his thighs swelled. Backboards were shattering like heads through windshields. Kids were bursting like squeezed cherry tomatoes.

When Mr. Bournesmith finally arrived, blood squirted from child ears and made squishing noises as Mr. Bournesmith's body expanded, bursting through jagged windowpanes, like water from a Fourth of July hose, with your thumb on the opening, maintaining the pressure, cold water running up your sleeve.

He opened his mouth.

Silly old Mr. Bournesmith, always getting himself into jams! Isn't that Mr. Bournesmith all over again: always opening his mouth and swallowing his own ears?

Plymouth Road Memoir

What was maddening on the Plymouth Road was the constant awareness that, though the majority of pilgrims one met along the road shared your conviction, it was possible to become someone new, born again, etc.; there was, nonetheless, a sizable minority struggling just as hard to hang on to who they always were, or more exactly, to be anyone at all. For every two Huck Finns, there was at least one Aunt Polly—and this was on the Plymouth Road, which anyone with any sense could see was a major thoroughfare among the backstreets at best, and hardly the main drag. It serves as a reminder to you that the Plymouth Road is important to you because it is slightly out of the way. It was celebrated because it was the road less traveled, and you loved it because just taking it made you feel different, unique, called.

It's no headline that the Plymouth Road never existed on any map, and, when roads appeared that were given the name, they weren't the same road you found yourself walking. This often led to great confusion, but sometimes enlightenment, as well. Once, along the road, I saw a shady crossroads leading to the orchard; it turned out to be the exit ramp to Ann Arbor. Not a bad place to be, but hardly the place where I was going.

The hard truth is that Huck was never welcome on Main Street, and the river just always rolled and never knew, or presumably cared, that it was named. You were on the Plymouth Road, and either you couldn't make it on Main Street, or you never could bring yourself to accept that Main Street was the only road to take, which pretty much amounted to the same thing.

The pilgrims on the Plymouth Road were all refugees, uprooted and displaced, the vast majority of whom would have just stayed home if they could have, and, yet, they just kept walking. Along the Plymouth Road. As if walking itself, leaving one's kindred, leaving one's land, going to a place I will show you, as if the sheer act of getting on board and needing no ticket were itself the fulfillment of a promise.

You met a lot of strange customers along the Plymouth Road, and you saw a lot of casualties along the way, and there were many nights you questioned your own judgment and longed for the cessation of the longing itself, but it wasn't like you didn't give thanks and rejoice with every step on the road, that narrow way, that royal road of dreams and faith.

That should be noted as well: the pilgrims who took to the Plymouth Road suffered the consequences of their choices, but at the same time received rare blessings and gifts, signs and portents of a time to come and a promised land—even discrete moments of ecstasy and release—that could never be found or savored on the main drag, though they only received those blessings and gifts in hardship and lack and squalor and humiliation. The road isn't for everyone, but it is there for those who need it—and that's one of the greatest lessons of the road itself: gratitude.

I wouldn't have had it any other way, which is why I always did penance on the Plymouth Road, always paid

my toll and peeled the onion—pay the man!— finding
the Rabbi always and only outside the camp.

I was walking down the Plymouth Road; it was me, the
Rabbi, and my brother, and we came upon a man who
operated the locks on some out-of-the-way—some no-
name—canal, which fed the system, the infrastructure—
the Erie Canal. And he pulled the levers, and he turned
the dials, and he opened gates and closed gates and
raised the water level and lowered the water level, and,
his whole life, he had allowed boats and barges to get to
where they were going, and goods to where they were
needed, and passage to some other place, some other
place, just get me the fuck out of here, on all those last-
chance American boats, last-chance American barges;
but he'd never been to Buffalo, never himself, left his
little station in Waterloo, NY—a way-station itself—a
backwater, a becalming, not properly a part of the Erie
Canal, though it could get you there, which was the
point. The Great Lakes.

And this man had spent his whole life making it
possible for other people to get where they were going
and goods where they were needed, and he'd never been
a damn place himself, just remained at his station, a
secondary station, feeding into the Erie Canal, so that
people and goods could get where they were going,
make passage, arrive finally and reliably, just that and
nothing else. And it was so very long after the railroads,
and so very long after the highway system, and so very
long after Wall Street and anyone caring.

And I said to the man, this is what I said, "Don't
you feel used?"

And he looked at me—he looked at me a long time—
like he was perplexed, like he was hearing a language he
used to speak, long ago, when he was young, long before

the stars fell from the sky, fell from the sky like ripe figs, and the heavens rolled up like a scroll.

And he said, this is what he said to me, "Does the nail complain because it's not a hammer?"

And I said, this is what I said, "Yeah, it does. It most certainly does."

And he said, "I'm not a nail, and neither are you."

And the Rabbi said nothing.

And my brother said nothing.

And I opened my mouth to say something, but I had nothing, and nothing came out.

The canal man pulled his levers and twisted his dials, and boats and barges got where they were going. The Great Lakes. The water flowed.

This hammer is so friggin' heavy.

The canal man didn't look up when I waved goodbye. Everyone was going home. The Great Lakes.

I was walking down the Plymouth Road, and I asked the Rabbi if it would get better.

I said, "It gets better, right?"

And he said, "Technically, it's never been any worse or any better."

"Yeah, but it gets better, right?"

"Your love has to grow bigger than your outrage."

"Oh, for Christ's sake!"

"Language, Pilgrim, language!"

"You probably think this is pretty funny, don't you?" I asked the Rabbi.

"Wouldn't you?" he asked in reply.

4

I was walking down the Plymouth Road, and all its edges were bleeding over. Homeric shades from down in the hole were approaching.

"Give us blood! Give us blood!" they were shrieking.

And then suddenly, they would turn into some guy in McCaffrey's telling me about this week's sale on pork loins. "It's a steal, dude."

It was unnerving, as if I could no longer manage the compartmentalizing of the two worlds, and a whole lot depended upon me keeping those two worlds straight.

The Rabbi was nowhere to be found. I was on my own. It was a real horror show.

Some lady named Berenice was trying to extract someone's teeth, and, out on the docks, they were doing things to Melville that were unspeakable. I witnessed the dissection of Hawthorne by several farm families at the Mercer County Library, and it was all done in the dark. Afterward, all the surgeons repaired to the traditional chicken pot pie dinner in Dutch Neck.

Ralph Waldo was there too, and his hair was on fire, and he was laughing hysterically, and he was quoting Scripture, "When I am weak, then I am strong.

When I am weak, then I am strong!" He was rubbing himself inappropriately in public and ruining his reputation.

Emerson on the Plymouth Road.

And yet, all the while, the other world—the straight world—was crashing in, and everybody was mowing their lawns and attending travel soccer matches and murmuring under their breath. They landed a space shuttle on the Intrepid in New York.

I cried out in my anger and my shame, "I am leaving! I am leaving!" but it just turned out to be another Paul Simon song.

"Had enough?" the Rabbi asked.

"Where the hell were you!" I screamed, unsettled by the depth of my own rage, the cliffs of the palisades collapsing into the Hudson.

"Where I go, you cannot follow," he said.

"You left me alone!"

"That's not even the half of it, Pilgrim."

"What do you expect from me?"

"Everything, and I'm not even here."

The erosion ceased. The world grew calm. Suddenly, nothing threatened on the Plymouth Road. The levee stopped breaking—Washington crossed the Delaware. All things being equal, I just settled down. Tending to the whiplash.

"You hungry?" the Rabbi asked. "I know a place down the road; they do a *chicken francese* that's to die for."

"They got fish and chips?"

"You know it son; they got fish."

"I'm so hungry. You think the levee's gonna hold?"

"Let's eat first and then see how we feel."

"I'm scared, Rabbi."

"This place I know, it's just around the bend. We're halfway there and back. We're practically there."

I kept walking, and I looked, but the Rabbi was nowhere to be found. The levee groaned. That's the way it was. Things kept going back and forth.

If you're hungry enough, you just keep walking, past the country clubs—alone, but not alone—past the full-scale invasions of column upon column of desire—with and without the Rabbi—who is always there, if not here—past the haunted mansions on the hill, past the subdivisions, past the howling banshees of loneliness in the heart of America—past the night-time, illuminated baseball diamonds, where all the pale ghosts demand their black blood behind home plate—past the bones of the pilgrims moldering in patriot graves on Bunker Hill and Haymarket Square, you just...around the bend, just around the bend...keep walking—with the crash on the levee always about to begin—and the reek of bombs—you just keep walking.

"What's it going to be, Pilgrim, the Chicken or the Fish?" the Rabbi asked, as the membrane melted and solidified—and the heavens forever threatened rain and you were not erased in the ambiguity.

"What's it going to be?"

As if maybe it was about time to get off the Plymouth Road and set some roots somewhere.

The Confidence Man
Explains the Long Con

God is always in the room you don't want to go into. He's waiting there for you. And you never want to open that door. All the pikers and hanger-ons, all the flimflam boys and faro dealers, they are always just going to give you permission to stay where you are, selling you the license to never open that door. They are selling you real estate you already own. They are collecting rent on your shackles. And most of the time you're happy to pay. Doesn't that beat all? We are all too happy to pay to avoid being who we are.

Okay, maybe calling it "God" is the problem. The scandal of particularity. It doesn't really matter what you call it. It's not like the atheist is ever going to avoid having to open that door. It's not like the door wouldn't be there, just waiting to be opened, if there weren't no God. What, do we have to speak baby-talk? God is never what we mean when we say "God." Duh! Jeeze Louise! Anyone who has ever felt awe knows that. Anyone who has ever loved and lost and lived to tell the tale knows that. You can't reduce these things to names. You can't tame the tempest in words.

For all intents and purposes, there's nothing but the door and the room you don't want to enter. And here's the thing, boys: It is all too easy to label what lies beyond the door, in the room we don't want to enter, "evil." It's red meat to politicians, priests, ministers, and clergy, the numbers-runners of our body politic. They got ways to make you turn your cowardice into virtue every which way to Sunday.

You got pulpit-pounders and shamans, Tarot card readers to the stars, you got prognosticators and mediums who channel the wisdom of lost masters in Atlantis. You got puritan divines and Catholic prelates. You got skeptics and debunkers, devotees of the cult of reason; you got professors and auto-didactics; you got the three-card-monte boys in Times Square and roulette dealers in Monte Carlo.

You got everything you need to justify not opening that damned door.

Jeeze Louise! It's not like you don't have to open it. I mean, it's not like it won't ever stop being there just waiting for you to open it. It's not like you don't have to take your own bath.

So what are you waiting for? Just open the damn door. Whatever is waiting for you there knows your true name. It's been waiting for you forever.

I was walking down the Plymouth Road, and I was pretty much done with it. I didn't want to play hide and seek anymore. I didn't want to be away from my family.

I had Mongo Santamaria playing in my earphones and visions I just couldn't use anymore. I was digging a hole to find the place where revelation met imagination, and everything around me just kept affirming my suspicion that you can't dig your way out of that hole.

Sooner or later, you're going to have to hoist your own damn sail and trust in the wind.

I had lunch with Wordsworth and Coleridge. They turned out to be a couple guys with their own responsibilities. It wasn't like they were going to ever help you move, even if you rented the van and promised them pizza and beer.

It was the same with Paul Ricoeur and Arthur Rimbaud and Hank Williams. Walt Whitman was dead, and Jack Kerouac was still blowing—blowing a cool wind all the way down from Baudelaire to Edgar Allan Poe, to Charlie Parker—but the clock was ticking, and it wasn't like I was getting any younger.

I am not anywhere other than where I have always struggled to arrive, exhausting my life the whole time. And maybe it's time to just be here.

I want to build something. I ain't no anarchist.

"You think you're ready?" the Rabbi asked.

"Not really," I replied.

"Lo, I am with you until the end of the age."

"That's funny because it's true and not true all at the same time."

"I never promised you a rose garden."

"You're just a laugh riot, aren't you?"

"As long as you keep laughing."

"Yeah. As long as I keep laughing."

No one said nothing.

"I'm scared, Rabbi."

"I'd be worried about you if you weren't."

"I'm just working on a building."

"A Holy Ghost building."

"Thank you."

"See you in your dreams, Pilgrim."

"Not if I see you first."

Morning dawned on Mercer County in Central New Jersey like it had been planned or something.

Series Two

1

I was walking down the Plymouth Road. Just the Rabbi and me. And after a while, we arrived. We arrived in Plymouth. And there just wasn't anything there. Not even a rock or a seagull.

"I guess we've gone about as far as we can go," I said to the Rabbi.

"I guess so," he said.

But it wasn't true. And both of us knew it.

"Is there any more of that beef jerky?" he asked.

"I think we ate the last of it an hour ago."

"You ready?"

"It's not like I have to be anywhere in the morning," I replied.

"Me neither," he said.

We just kept walking.

On May 18th, 1926, Aimee Semple McPherson—Sister Aimee—Radio Evangelist—Faith Healer—Four-Square Gospel—first woman ever in the U.S.A. to get a broadcast license—Sister Aimee—built the Angelus Temple in Echo Park, Los Angeles—yes, *that* Sister! On May 18th, 1926, Sister Aimee entered the Pacific Ocean north of Venice Beach, California and disappeared. She was with her secretary. In the search, parishioners drowned in the surf.

About the same time, her married Radio Engineer, Kenneth G. Ormiston, disappeared. The two of them were subsequently seen together in apparent scenes of great amorousness, all up and down the West Coast.

On June 23rd—about a month later—Sister Aimee emerged from the desert alone in Agua Prieta, Mexico, just across the border from Douglas, Arizona. This is 1926 we're talking about here. She was wearing slippers. And they were not scuffed. But they sure were grass-stained.

Quite the scandal.

She claimed she had been kidnapped, tortured. Claimed she was held for ransom in a desert shack by desperate customers: "Steve" and the gun moll, "Mexicali Rose," and some unknown man. She escaped. She emerged from the desert with grass-stained slippers after having walked thirteen hours.

Out of the sea and into the desert.

"This is how one pictures the angel of history. His face is turned toward the past...The angel would like to stay, awaken the dead, and make whole what has been smashed. But a storm is blowing from Paradise; it has

got caught in his wings with such violence that the angel can no longer close them. The storm irresistibly propels him into the future to which his back is turned...This storm is what we call progress."
—Walter Benjamin

I was walking down the Plymouth Road. It was me and the Rabbi. But it wasn't really the same. We'd arrived at our destination. But we kept walking. So I didn't really know what road we were on. I kind of broached the subject with him. The Rabbi.

"Remember what you said?" I asked him. "I mean, about the end of the age?"

"You mean, 'Lo, I will be with you'?"

"Yeah."

"What about it?"

"Well..."

"Are you worried that the age is ending and I won't be there on the other side?" he asked.

"Well, I wouldn't exactly put it that way, but..."

There was an awkward silence.

"So, let me get this straight..."

"You don't have to get your nose all bent out of joint," I said.

"No, no, let me just make sure I know what you're saying..."

"C'mon now, you're obviously pissed."

"I'm not pissed!"

"We've been together for a long time, I think I know when you're pissed," I said.

"Oh, so now you can read my mind?"

"Don't be like that..."

"Be like what? No, really, I'd like to know. Be like what?"

"C'mon now, I didn't mean anything."

"Well, if you didn't mean anything, why did you say anything?"

"I just...I mean..."

"Psych!" The Rabbi started to laugh.

"What?"

"I really had you going there!"

"You probably think you're pretty funny, don't you?"

"Not as funny as you."

We just walked a while in silence.

"Then the Lord rained on Sodom and Gomorrah sulfur and fire from the Lord out of heaven; and he overthrew those cities, and all the Plain, and all the inhabitants of the cities, and what grew on the ground.
But Lot's wife, behind him, looked back, and she became a pillar of salt."
Genesis 19:24-26

"Rabbi...."

"Don't worry about it. I've got your back."

"I know but...."

"Listen, the only thing that's ever going to get in the way of you and me is your fear."

"But I'm so frightened..."

"Don't freak out. You still think I'm funny, right?"

"Well, you do crack me up..."

"Then you're good. The only thing that kills fear is laughter."

"I thought it was love."

"Same difference."

"Rabbi...where are we going?"

"That's the question, isn't it?"
"You're not as funny as you think."
"Yes, I am," he said.

After a brief but dark time in New Jersey, I found myself back in the Michigan of my youth. Not Ann Arbor, but Lansing. Such is the nature of actual places—places where people live—the distinction matters. University of Michigan versus Michigan State. Stuck-up assholes versus the rest of us.

By all objective measures, I had landed on my feet. A high-steeple church with a heart. In Lansing.

Sometimes though, in the middle of the night, I would wake up in a panic. I could feel my memories eroding. I could feel the Michigan of my dreams—the Michigan of my childhood—so much milkweed—being replaced with new images and new memories, and I was bereft—oddly, but firmly, bereft.

I was walking down the Plymouth Road. It was me and the Rabbi. And we'd come to the part of our journey where we had arrived, but still needed to keep going. I saw in my mind's eye an oval, an undulating and lovely oval. I imagined we had arrived within the oval. Breached the perimeter. Outrun the demons. We had arrived in the neutral place. Zero. Without sight. We walked and made progress, but never left the oval. We kept going, but never left where we always were. Ground Zero.

The landscape of the soul is not that of the ego. We live dual lives. The ego goes its own way. The way of the soul is another.

"Okay," I said, "I think I get it."

"Well," the Rabbi said, "if you think you get it, then you pretty much missed the point."

We walked a while in silence. But I could see that the Rabbi was pleased.

"I love you, Rabbi," I said.

"I love you too, Pilgrim," he said.

The oval. The Zero. It was dancing. The mountains clapped their hands, and the sea—in this case, Lake Michigan—sang.

I was walking down the Plymouth Road with the Rabbi, and I could not trust the neutral place. Did not know Zero. I could not lay my burden down. I could not surrender. Could not study war no more.

I was freaking out. I was having a moment. I was being a drama king. The Rabbi just stood there. I vomited all over his sandals:

I remember hitchhiking from Ohio to South Dakota with the girl with Campbell Soup calves. Made it all the way to Deadwood. It was in the spring, and the Great Plains announced itself, as the great scroll was unrolled across the horizon. The grass was tall and red as the wind blew until it felt like you were watching the motion of waves—some ghost of the great ocean that once covered this land—grass waving like seaweed. I had seen the movement of reeds in shallow Midwestern lakes. I recognized the rhythm.

I remember soaking dried cattails in gasoline and marching with torches on eighth-grade nights. I remember the creative need to destroy. I marched around the walls of Jericho in Illinois. In Michigan.

I remember stepping out of a subway into a pool of blood on the streets of New York. I remember the dead man on the street. And the sudden flurry of cops. I remember the bloody footprints on 110th Street and how they were mine—as I went my way.

I remember the way the wide-open-ness of the Illinois prairie struck me as holy and lonely as a child and now strikes me as a provocation. I remember dragging dying mama-rabbits home and tending the babes in the nest after she died. I remember smashing the head of a rabbit after I had hit it with the car and its back was broken and it was screaming and the amount of force I used with the stone to just stop it forever. Stop the screaming.

I remember the great loneliness and the way that trees could stop the eye and the imagination.

I remember snot-freezing-cold winter mornings when your hair freezes while you are waiting for the bus. I remember waiting for my Dad to pick me up after wrestling practice in Plymouth, Michigan and the sun has gone down and looking up at the stars and the sudden vertigo as I am night-sky-swallowed and suddenly know my God. My Rock. The Fear of Isaac.

I remember the sound of bug-zappers and lust—desire executed in the night—down by the new ball park with white concrete and wire-link fences. I remember how desire was given the chair and just came back, like it was indestructible, like there was Resurrection calling out around the world in America.

And the softness of a young girl's lips and the blossom of Cezanne and Geometry.

I remember the delight of innocence. The license of innocence. I remember the overwhelming cleanliness. The preening and the exaltation.

I remember the great humor and the gales of laughter and the great hunger. I remember the sadness of gum wrappers—in bicycle-wheel tracks—in springtime mud—full of rainwater.

I remember the sound of God walking in the garden and how even the terror was delightful. I remember singing hymns that made the world turn and made graves be opened on a dreary Sunday morning.

I remember all that was lost and the knowledge that there were things lost I couldn't even begin to imagine.

I remember. I remember. I remember.

Angel of History. Spinning like a weathervane. Janie's got a gun. Just got to purge. Again and again. Out of the sea and into the desert.

Had to vomit on the Rabbi's sandals. Adam's apple all a-tremble. All this life. Stuck in my craw. Stuck in my heart.

2

I was walking in place with the Rabbi down the Plymouth Road, and we came upon the Cities on the Plain. They were frozen in catastrophe as if History itself had paused in the very moment of disaster. There were two cities, but their names were unclear and inadequately translated. The first was the City of the Distracted, and the second was the City of the Agitated.

In the City of the Distracted, there were no living creatures at all, just structures on the lip of collapse. Architecture. Nothing but doomed buildings, virtual Towers of Babel—a fraction of an instant before they were destroyed.

In the City of the Agitated, there was nothing but creatures in panic. History itself had stopped, but the inhabitants remained in motion, running hither and yon, back and forth, across busy thoroughfares; the city itself had become the Condition of Terror.

In the first City on the Plain, the City of the Distracted, the Rabbi and I played soccer in the empty and hollow streets. (He won, three goals to two.) In the second City on the Plain, the City of the Agitated, the Rabbi and I met up with the underground resistance and helped to reinforce the barricades. We installed sleeper cells, a holy remnant, to secure the future after the catastrophe. Each member of each cell worked independently; none of the freedom fighters knew one another—it was deemed too dangerous. Thirty-Six Zadikim.

We were walking, but we were walking in place. Always having arrived, but never finished with the journey. Always aware of the potential for the reek of bombs.

"I'm not quite sure I understand what's going on here," I said to the Rabbi.

"You've got to spread your bets around, Pilgrim. Can't put all your eggs in one basket."

"I have no idea what you're talking about."

"History is only a chapter in the Book of Life, and that book has always been written, but it is never finished. Got it?"

"No."

"Never mind, it doesn't really require your understanding."

The catastrophe hit. The Cities on the Plain were destroyed.

The Rabbi and I walked away with a soccer ball and the addresses of three safe-houses. We just kept walking, dancing on graves and planting vineyards.

"History does not forgive," the Rabbi said. "And the vanquished will always return. And you've got to be ready, Pilgrim."

"I'm not kidding," he added for emphasis.

In 1919, the people of Centralia, Washington, should have been happy. The war to end all wars was over. The boys were home. But the people of Centralia in 1919 were full of dread and revulsion.

Maybe it was what the boys had seen. What the boys had done. Over there.

They had not saved civilization. Not made the world safe for democracy. They had been trapped in trenches in a slaughterhouse. And they had done things that they had no Christian words for. And they were not all right, those boys. They were full of rage. Full of the need to erase. To release. Forget. And they were looking for someone to pay. Somebody had to pay. For this horror. This unholy thing that they had become. Pay for being beyond the circle of belonging.

I suppose it's not really surprising that, when the Legionnaires marched on the first anniversary of Armistice Day in Centralia, Washington, in 1919, they decided to raid the offices of the IWW—Industrial Workers of the World—or the "I Won't Work" crowd as the boys called it. It wasn't surprising. The Wobblies had refused the role they'd been given. Found it too constraining. They were looking for something more. They were vagrants.

What was surprising was that the Wobblies were waiting when the Legionnaires came to smash their windows, break up their furniture, and tar and feather any IWW man they could find. This time, the Wobblies were waiting, and they had guns.

That surely did surprise the Legionnaires and the people of Centralia. People who were looking forward to dealing with their problems.

When the Legionnaires broke down the door to the offices of the IWW, Wesley Everest came out shooting. Shots were coming from everywhere, but Wesley came out through the smashed-in door. Gun in each hand like some Hollywood gangster from the 30s. Gats ablazing. You'll never get me alive, copper!

But they did get him alive. Cornered him at the river. He turned to face the mob before it got to him. And then he fired right into it. Fired into the mob. Killed one of the pack. And then they descended on Wesley Everest and beat the shit out of him.

They beat him because he'd killed one of the pack. Because they were full of dread and revulsion. Because it was Armistice Day. Like he thought he was better than them.

When they were done beating him, they took him to the jailhouse. They'd already rounded up all the rest of the Wobblies they could catch. Took him to the jailhouse and threw him on the floor in a cell crowded with other beaten Wobblies, where he lay groaning, unable to move.

Outside the jailhouse, the crowds were gathering. The surprise was beginning to wear off and was turning to something else. Outside the jailhouse there were mothers and fathers, children and old men, veterans and clergymen. People of Centralia. Just folks.

The crowds gathered, and then they attacked. Just folks. Broke down the door. Smashed into the cell. Grabbed Wesley Everest. They weren't finished with him. They grabbed his limp, still-breathing, beaten body and put a rope around his neck.

When they got to the bridge, they tied one end of the rope to the railing and threw Wesley off. He jerked around a little, and they realized the rope wasn't long enough to break his neck, so they hauled him up again.

Someone went to get a longer rope. They tied one end to the railing and the other to the noose around Wesley's neck. Then, they threw him over again.

But they weren't finished. When the people of Centralia were done throwing Wesley Everest off the bridge and watching him swing around on the end of the line, they all climbed down and went to the riverbank and emptied their guns into his body. They fired until there were no more bullets.

When the people of Centralia were done shooting at Wesley's body from the riverbank, they retrieved him, smashed in his teeth with a rifle butt, and castrated him. When the people of Centralia were done, Wesley Everest was dead. Like he'd never been born.

I was walking down the Plymouth Road. It was just me and the Rabbi. But it wasn't like the Devil had just given up. He kept trying to intrude, permeate the perimeter of the dancing oval. The Zero.

I started to laugh because he was making no headway. I pointed my finger at him and danced a victory dance. But the Rabbi rebuked me.

He wrote a Holy Name in the sand and breached the oval, the Holy Zero, and he invited the Devil in.

"What are you doing?" I asked.

He didn't even bother to respond.

The Devil hovered around the breach, but he would not enter the oval, the Holy Zero. Instead, the Devil wept and gnashed his teeth. He keened and added his voice to the great howl, the great sorrow. But he could not enter the oval. He could not cross that Rubicon. He could not violate the perimeter. The price was just too great.

He wept an entire river of tears. Entrepreneurs created ferry businesses and made a killing. But the Devil couldn't cross. Or wouldn't. He sat on the banks of the river he had created and wept. River of tears.

I looked at the Rabbi.

We were on the Plymouth Road. The Rabbi and I (and the Cloud of Witnesses) surrounding us. All of us together. Like it was Old Home Week.

"Rabbi?"

"Yes, Pilgrim."

"Is it just me or has everything been turning into its opposite and then turning back again? I mean, for quite a while now?"

"You'll get used to it."

"I'll take that as a 'yes?'"

"What, you thought this would be straightforward?" he asked.

"No, I guess not."

We kept walking.

"Rabbi?"

"Yes, Pilgrim."

But I had nothing.

When I was a child, I had a remarkable lack of confidence that if I kept going around the block I would inevitably return to where I had started. Bad sense of direction. Each turn, at every corner, presented a new story, a new world, a new map. No home. No continuity.

We just walked—me, the Rabbi, and the Cloud of Witnesses. And after a while, I just lost myself in the company—keeping company—and was not afraid that I would be unable to find my way back.

We just walked.

Home is where the closed door is always open.

"Pilgrim?"

"Yeah?"

"You should maybe take off your shoes. This is Hallowed Ground."

"Yeah, you're right."

I took them off.

The dust was warm.

And I was not consumed.

3

I was walking in place with the Rabbi down the Plymouth Road and came upon a natural theater in the woods. There was a summer stock touring company scheduled to perform. They were putting on a Cecil B. Demille spectacle. Real Hill Commorah stuff. Or maybe Oberammergau.

The Rabbi and I—well, we could've used a diversion—an infusion. We stopped to see the show.

The show opened with a mud creature that had been given the breath of life. The original Golem. The playwright archly had given the mud creature the name of "Adam."

Anyway, in the show, Adam and Eve—I mean, the two come together—sat outside the gates of the Orchard, entrance made impossible by flaming swords. (Between you and me, the special effects were a little alarming. An open flame in an outdoor theater? With this drought?! No one seemed to notice or to care.)

Anyway, the audience was meant to know that the mud creature and his "bone of his bone and flesh of his flesh" were meant to know that they could pass through the gates of the Orchard if they were True. The False, however, could not enter the gates.

Every year at an appointed time, Adam and Eve would come to the gates and supplicate themselves. They would purge themselves. Make themselves naked. They would become authentic. Pure. True. And every year they would be rejected at the Gates of the Orchard.

This was not some cheap propaganda from the Head Office. The Diocese. The General Assembly. This was the kind of theater that meant business.

Year after year, it was the same: they would come, they would strip off what was not necessary. They would become Pure. True. And year after year, they were refused entry. Until the final year. The last year. The Denouement.

At the end of the age, Adam and Eve arrived at the appointed time. They donned ridiculous costumes and wigs and false teeth. They came in disguise. And did not pretend to hide it. They became false.

And the gates opened wide. And Adam and Eve entered the Orchard.

The Curtain fell. The crowd of misfits and losers, rejects and dead-enders, tax-collectors and prostitutes—well, they just went wild. Gave a standing ovation that lasted for years.

It takes a special kind of person to acknowledge the bullshit—especially if it's your own.

Still, if you want to know the truth, I was kind of offended by the performance. The implications! I turned to the Rabbi, to get some affirmation. Am I wrong?

But when I turned to look at him, he just kept pulling his face off. Layer upon layer. It was turtles all the way down.

He was laughing, but not at me. Just peeling his face off like an onion. All the way to Infinity and back.

Alright, I'll give him that—when I settled down, I had to admit—it was kind of funny.

Still, I was unnerved by the whole thing. The layers upon layers of face. And it peeling like an onion.

"What?" the Rabbi asked. "You pissed at me?"

"Sometimes, you expect too much!" I shouted, the spit spraying from my lips.

"Yeah, but you still think it's funny, don't you?"

I threw a half-eaten box of popcorn at his face. He ducked.

I couldn't help myself. I burst out laughing and sobbing. Both at the same time. Tears and laughter.

The Rabbi held me until I regained my composure.

The Rabbi was not a cruel man.

"To reach satisfaction in all
desire its possession in nothing.
To come to possession in all
desire the possession of nothing.
To arrive at being all
desire to be nothing.
To come to the knowledge of all
desire the knowledge of nothing.
To come to the pleasure you have not
you must go by the way in which you enjoy not.
To come to the knowledge you have not
you must go by the way in which you know not.

> To come to the possession you have not
> you must go by the way in which you possess not.
> To come by the what you are not
> you must go by a way in which you are not.
> When you turn toward something
> you cease to cast yourself upon the all.
> For to go from all to the all
> you must deny yourself of all in all.
> And when you come to the possession of the all
> you must possess it without wanting anything.
> Because if you desire to have something in all
> your treasure in God is not purely your all."
> —St. John of the Cross

"Is this truly what is required?" I asked.

"Required? We're getting to the point where that's kind of beside the point."

"Is there any way out?"

"Out? Pilgrim, it's all about the way in. It's always been about the way in."

"I—"

"Just be quiet. I mean, for once, just shut up."

"For your own good," he added after a while.

I opened my mouth, and entire silences came out. And it was glorious and beautiful and moving. I lost control of my fine motor control. I throbbed. My paper-thin hands fluttered; my knees buckled. Feeling faint. God-swallowed. I waited it out. Lack of oxygen to the brain.

The return of desire in the abdication of desire.

I regained my composure.

Everything and nothing had changed.

"The heavens are telling the glory of God;
and the firmament proclaims his handiwork.
Day to day pours forth speech,
and night to night declares knowledge.
There is no speech, nor are there words; their voice is
not heard;
yet their voice goes out through all the earth,
and their words to the end of the world."
Psalm 19:1-4

I regained composure. And then I lost it, again.

Pierced in the side with a dart of longing. Hot blood and water splashing and steaming on the stage.

I was walking in place down the Plymouth Road with the Rabbi, and we came upon *El Santuario de Chimayo*. New Mexico. Land of Enchantment. Abandoned crutches and braces cluttered the way. The air smelled of rust, dried blood, and horror. The air smelled of dust, thorns, and healing.

It seems a memorial service was about to take place. The congregation was gathering. Ghosts and pilgrims along the Plymouth Road. We decided to stop. It is a good thing to remember the saints.

A slightly stylized version of myself dressed with vestments made of buckskin and fringe stepped up to the pulpit to give the eulogy as we took our seats.

"This isn't right," I said to the Rabbi.

"What do you mean?" he asked.

"I look like Kit Carson!" I protested.

"What makes you think that that's you?"

"Oh, Jeeze Louise! Anybody can see that that's me!"

"I don't see the resemblance."

"For Christ's sake!"

"Really, Pilgrim? Haven't I told you a thousand times to watch your language? Anyway, would you please be quiet? I want to hear what the preacher has to say."

I bit my tongue. Listened to the preacher. And this is what he said:

Carl Bisson was from Maine. He lived on West End Avenue on the Upper West Side, in a comfortable and cavernous apartment somewhere in the 90s. He was an Elder in the Church. A Godly man. And a bit of a lech.

In some ways, in those days—mid 80s—NYC seminary days—in the days when AIDS hit the gay community like a stroke, leaving it hobbled and hamstrung—heartbroken and humiliated—like a crippled horse—in some ways, he was a throwback to the wicked, old, and hungry days of the chiselers and nancy boys, of those orgiastic days of forbidden bathhouses—and shame. And in other ways, in those days, he was like a lonesome pilgrim—poor wayfaring stranger—returning from a future most longed for—a Marco Polo of the heart—Marco! Polo!—bringing tidings of a home where every tear is dried and every sorrow turned to dancing—and every turning terminated.

Carl showed up once to a Bible Study at the church, absurd in his leathers. Though he was in his 40s, he was hopeful till the end that he would remain the mysterious stud, and that eventually all the beautiful boys would once and for all fall to their knees in adoration and astonished recognition. He explained that, after the Bible Study, he had an appointment with love at a leather bar in the Village. We groaned and giggled when he waggled his dentures, suggesting that there were advantages for a man of his inclinations with no teeth.

I, of course, was shocked and scandalized. From where I came—and in fact, from where Carl came too, though many years and miles apart—from Michigan to Maine—one did not walk in transparency or affirm what must be denied in the face of "decency" and "folks just like us." Carl, in New York City, wasn't like any "us" I knew but, nonetheless, danced before the LORD like the light of candlesticks on the Common Table on Communion Sundays, when all God's children got courage.

When I was scared and out of my league, Carl took me under his wing and showed me how to visit the dying in hospitals—how to touch the AIDS lepers with such faith and gentleness that in the touch itself, there was nothing for all us poor bastards to do but behold the face of the Christ in the poor and be at peace. Carl, in my suffocating Midwesternisms, Carl in New York City, taught me to be a Pastor. Carl was kind.

Carl is dead now. I went to his funeral. And I miss him something fierce. I wish, now that I am again scared and out of my league, that he would take me to lunch at his favorite diner right there on Broadway, where they have the handsome waiters and a good Monte Cristo, and teach me to remember again what I've always known in the great illiterate silence of my salvation—always known, but always forgotten—like the sound of your own name repeated until you got no words, just sounds that lean toward meaning.

Teach me to remember what I have always known:

We are loved.

And that is enough.

Good night, sweet Carl.

The lights came up, and the congregation began to disperse. I didn't know what to say. I didn't have any words. As I had watched the preacher speak, I had watched myself appear and disappear. A flickering wick. My whole life captured in an attempt to light a cigarette in the wind.

I felt a loneliness that was bigger than me, older than me. A light shining in the darkness. A light not overcome by the darkness. A light that could not be seen without the darkness. A simple light. Illuminating the Rabbi's face. A simple loneliness.

I turned to him, but he had already turned to me. And I beheld his face.

And Carl said to me—this is what he said:

"Good night, Pilgrim."

And I said—this is what I said:

"Good night, Carl."

And then the Rabbi and I kept walking, down the Plymouth Road, lined with abandoned braces and crutches—the spent whips of *Los Hermanos Penitentes*—and the brutal tenderness of *Los Flagelantes*.

"Good night, Rabbi," I said.

"Good night, Pilgrim," he said.

As we walked into the setting sun, rejoicing and giving praise.

Through streets of blood.

SERIES THREE
THE GREAT REFUSAL

To live outside the law you must be honest
I know you always *say* that you agree.
Bob Dylan, 1966

I was walking down the Plymouth Road, and it was me and the Rabbi, and we came across the silence. It rolled like fog on a Southern Tier morning. Upstate New York. I stepped out into the silence and disappeared. The Rabbi came with me. And we disappeared.

The silence became visible. It was like fog. When you're venturing beyond your range of knowledge. Like you're driving your Ford Escort in the fog. And your headlights reflect. And there is whiteout.

I remember driving between Waterloo, New York, and my folks' home in Rochester. This would have been in the late eighties / early nineties. Upstate New York. Finger Lakes region. I remember driving my old, black Ford Escort. Lake effect snow. On one side of the New York State Thruway, there would be a foot of snow, and, on the other, nothing. Driving. Snowflakes as big as the reflectors on poles on the Thruway.

The driving was like dancing. I knew every curve and turn of the road. I knew when to accelerate in the curve and when to change lanes.

Silence. Sounds absorbed. Homecoming. In the silence. In the whiteout. We always were driving blind and always blind to arrivals. I only just now was coming to really understand that. In the fullness of my dialectic.

Me and the Rabbi.

"You crack me up, Pilgrim," the Rabbi said.

"Yeah. I'm glad I amuse you."

"You see far, but are blind to what is close up."

"Well, I don't make any apologies for either the fog or the snow. I mean, isn't that what you taught me? You've just got to ride these things out?"

"You ride out what you don't create. You own what you do."

"What's that supposed to mean?"

"There is no silence, just a great refusal."

"You really want to go there? You really want to take that away from me?"

"Yes."

"I think you credit me with too much."

"No. I don't."

The fog grew thick and then thicker. The silence deepened. In my old Ford Escort, I careened on the Plymouth Road through early morning fog in the hills of the Southern Tier. Through snowstorms on I-90, trying to get home, the snow blotting out the road.

"You want to make me responsible for all this."

"I want to make you responsible."

"I can't handle the guilt."

"I just want you to handle the road; you're going to kill us if you keep on like this."

"I've got nothing left."

"Nevertheless."

"I got nothing to say."

"Never stopped you before."

I was so angry I couldn't even look at the Rabbi.

But he looked at me. And I melted.

"I can't do this."

"It doesn't really matter, Pilgrim."

I didn't say anything for a real long time. Silence. And then: "Yeah."

"You mad at me?" he said after a while.

"Yeah, but you'll be there on the other side, right?"

"Like water going downhill."

"I love you, Rabbi."

"I love you too, Pilgrim."

"This is going to suck."

"Pretty much."

The silence deepened. Snowflakes fell. Fog rolled in. The great refusal loomed on the blank horizon. As I parked my old Ford Escort on the side of the road. And just got out.

And walked.

I was walking down the Plymouth Road with the Rabbi, and we came to an exit for the Orchard.

Four pilgrims sat on the exit ramp and would not take it. Would not take the exit. We fell in with them. Thick as thieves. Me and the Rabbi. They just sat there as if in protest. Four pilgrims. A sit-down strike. At the exit ramp. And they wouldn't exit, or enter, the Orchard. The great refusal.

We sat down with them at the gates of the Orchard. Me and the Rabbi, trying our best to swallow a bad case of the giggles. We sat with the four pilgrims at the gates. And there was nothing funnier than these guys. Their ridiculousness. So close to home and perversely refusing to enter therein. Dying of thirst, two feet from the well. Funniest thing I ever saw.

Then, the first pilgrim stood up, entered the gates, saw the Orchard, and died.

The second pilgrim immediately stood up, entered the gates, saw the Orchard, and went mad. He returned to us, but he wasn't there. We chained him up for his own protection, but, in his lunacy, he broke the chains and made his dwelling in the caves and tombs. His body was wracked and rent by great sobs and the heavings of a sea of sorrow, like a herd of swine panicked and driven over a cliff.

The third pilgrim stood up, entered the gates, saw the Orchard, and cursed God. He found an axe and chopped down each and every tree in the Orchard. In his labors, his hands became stained with the sap of the trees of the Orchard. And the sap of the trees of the Orchard turned to blood. And it would never wash out.

Stained for the rest of his life. His hands. Stained with blood.

While he watched, one by one, the trees he had cut down return and sprout, and grow and bloom.

Finally, the fourth pilgrim stood up in peace. And entered the gates in peace. And departed in peace.

"You saw that, right?" the Rabbi asked.

"Yeah, I saw it," I said.

"What lesson can be learned?"

"Wait your turn?"

"Very good, Pilgrim. You're making progress."

"Thanks."

"Don't mention it."

We sat at the gates of the Orchard, longing, waiting, and fearing the coming of our turn. The inevitable and inexorable coming of our turn.

"Well," I said, "at least we can go together."

"What do you mean 'we,' kemosabe?"

It was funny in the way that it healed as it cut. It was funny.

But it wasn't that funny.

Michigan. My mother called Thursday afternoon. It's springtime. I'm up north in Ludington on Lake Michigan, for a week of study leave. Got elected to be a reader of Ordination Exams for the Denomination. Theology exams, to be exact (there are five total exams required for Ordination). Turns out that this time there was an abnormally low number of exams to be read. Lots of time to think. To be. To breathe. Up north.

So anyway, my mother called me up north. My mother never calls. She called because my father has been diagnosed with early stages of dementia. There is short-term memory loss. Irretrievable words. Houston, we have a problem. Seems my father neglected to pay a certain important bill. That was the last straw. So off to the VA they went. Had scans and such. Sure enough. Early stages of dementia. And all that that entails.

My father is a proud man.

My mother is prouder and more terrified. Quite out of character for her, she is openly operatic in her fear. Airing her dirty laundry for all to see. Almost enraptured in her debasement, like a character in a Dostoyevsky novel.

My sister is blooming late. Really coming into her own. After having withered in the shadow of our mother. She's divorced now, and the kids are all grown up. Two out of the three have moved to Denver, and the third is on his way—once he gets out of the Navy. My sister's selling her house in Rochester, Upstate New York, and moving to Denver. To be with the family. Family is everything.

Who gets to define family? Who gets to draw boundaries? Who is authorized to draw maps? And why do we all just keep getting erased?

My mother is guilting her shamelessly. My sister is resisting. My mother called to get me on her side. My sister is standing up. My mother wants me to tell my sister to move to Idaho. Take care of our parents. I am proud of my sister. Run, sister, run! Beat the shadow. Wants me to tell my sister to do her duty. Honor your father and mother.

My mother and my sister have been calling. Each one trying to get me on their side. A weapon against the other.

I have spent most of my life carefully sculpting all edges so that no one could get a purchase. I understood early on, with my father's approval, that if you didn't get out, they would suck you in. The shadow permeates and kills.

My father doesn't have any edges. Smooth. Like turtle wax. A good guide. Role model. My father never got sucked in, but left the women in the family resentful and barren. Non-generative. He lived the life he needed to live. He left Grangeville, Idaho, and made something of himself. Never looked back. Turned his back. Cold. Decisive. Don't look back. (Except that you always do.) There is a virtue in leaving the family and the land for a higher calling.

It's the women who pay. Like Dido.

Of course, after having turned his back on Idaho, my father needed to return for the last chapter of his life. Insisted that they return. Retired there. Idaho. Scene of his earliest memories, not my mother's. First

Lewiston and now Boise. Left my sister and the grandkids back in Rochester. Upstate New York. And cursed the city and the state on their way out. Rochester. New York State. Where they lived for over twenty years. Made it my sister's fault that they had to leave. Her fault that roots must be ripped. Out. Again. Abandoned my sister and her kids.

Here's the long and short of it: in order to leave Upstate New York, my mother had to foul the nest. Cursed the land and all its inhabitants. Deliberately hurt my sister. Demeaned her. Broke her. Just like when we were teenagers. Before Mother left with her man. Again.

The women in the family. Those two. They do things to each other that....

They betray each other for the men. Make each other pay for the price they pay to be the women. I don't want to be a man in this movie. I don't want to be a man to these women.

My father and I have not spoken of his dementia. We both know that the women have kept me informed. You don't have to say everything out loud. Seventy-eight years old. My father only wants to hear details about my success here, in Michigan. He triumphs in my triumphs. He relives his own in mine. Apart from the women.

My father is a proud man. He abandoned everything to become who he was created to be. Ripped out the roots. And turns out, it was the women who ended up paying.

Somebody always pays.

When my father's parents were dying, he wouldn't let either my sister or my mother be involved. Wouldn't let them help. They raged and rioted. He wouldn't let them in. They howled and keened and roamed the night with violence. They never forgave him.

I understood immediately. He couldn't trust what he loved to the women. They would drag it down. Make it ugly. And they would have. It's true. But I've lived long enough to know that he engineered that, too. He determined their roles. He left them nothing and drove them mad with love.

Absence and the great refusal. They are connected.

I am more like my father than I like to admit.

As I watch him turn his back to the land. And leave. Whiteout. Belligerently cheerful. In slow motion. Always already having gone. Going, going, gone.

(Did you see me wave, Dad? Do you feel the weight of my standing upon your shoulders? Are you scared? Will you let us hold the string to your kite? Will you fly away? *I'll fly away, oh glory, I'll fly away / When I die, Hallelujah, by and by / I'll fly away.* But you won't just fly away, will you, Dad? Are you scared? Dad, I'm scared. Will you let us be strong for you, like you were strong for us?)

If the women make me a man, can I find a way to be to them the man I actually am, or must I put on the mask of the father, the mask of the one who hurts them, yet is not destroyed by them? The women.

And what if the mask of the man I actually am is the same as my father's mask?

My grandfathers, on both sides of the family, left their mothers to broken fathers, and rode the rails during the Great Depression, uprooted and unmoored. Their ability to survive was their ability to leave no edges, turtle wax, lest anyone get a purchase.

This America with all its promise and all its heartbreak. All these American men and the women who paid the price for being American. The price for being free. Uprooted. Unmoored. In a never-ending now.

All these women in the American silence.

May God grant me the strength to be a son and a brother. And a husband.

After the Roller Coaster

My face feathered now with gold plate. My body a perfect gondola. The great water ride.

Horse and rider lost in the sea. The children of Israel cross over on dried land. To the other side. The click click click of the chain.

And we all go down.

I am an ark. A hollow vessel. Home of ghosts. I am who you will be after you take the ride. I am who you are when you rise from the dead. And stink. Death clinging to you.

I am the smell of cotton candy. I am the terror of the freak show. I am your mother and your father. I am everything you will never, ever, ever outrun.

Raise your hands, kids! Smile for the camera! We're going down!

The image of my face burnt in toast. My feet as fleet. As the sound of. The speed of. The loneliness of. It's all about getting goods from point A to point B, y'all! The trippers of the light fantastic.

I am before you and after you. After the roller coaster. I am the one always waiting for you just around the corner. I am. Always waiting. For you.

"Now faith is the assurance of things hoped for, the
conviction of things not seen."
—Hebrews 11:1

I do not believe in utopia, and yet I am animated by
utopian dreams. I am compelled to reach for what I do
not believe in. What I know to be a contradiction in
terms. An impossibility.

And yet I believe. And bear witness as the walls of
hostility, which I myself have erected, come a-tumbling
down, tumbling down, in my belief.

Do I create what is not in my longing, in my
hunger, in my conviction? In my need for it? Am I the
change I am looking for? Is to reach, in and of itself,
somehow, some kind of license? The proof of the theory
that gets the fly out of the bottle? Does my desire
provoke a response? My longing invoke the very word
of God?

"See, I am sending my messenger ahead of you,
who will prepare your way...."
Mark 1:2

Are we our own messengers, and why didn't Moses get
to enter the Promised Land?

Have I been so stupid for so long? Form is
emptiness is form is emptiness is....Have we been living
in utopia all along and not known it? No place. Dying
of thirst, two feet from the well? Is the Kingdom of God
in our midst? Is this hallowed ground and we failed to
take off our shoes?

Have I been wasting my tears?

Could it be that we are not only exiles but creators? And that the fulfillment of the Kingdom of God is in our hunger for it?

One foot in this world. One foot in the other.

Have I missed the love up close in seeking the love from afar?

And at the very least, can we distill ourselves into a holy remnant when the Tree of Life is cut down and the root of Jesse is exposed?

And when the very stones cry out in joy, do we even have a choice?

I was a sophomore in high school and wrestling on the Junior Varsity team at 98 pounds. In Plymouth, Michigan. I was small for my age and in my freshman year I had to gain weight to make 98 pounds. By my sophomore year, I had to watch my weight: I was inching up toward 103.

As Junior Varsity, at practice, you wrestled with the Varsity guys in your weight class. There was this guy. Sophomore year. We're talking late 70s here. I can see him so clearly but can't remember his name. I keep thinking "Joey." But Joey was this other guy, captain of the team, feathered hair, and a Smokey-and-the-Bandit-Trans-Am on his 16th birthday. You never said it out loud, but everybody knew that Joey's Dad was Mafia. Joey almost went to jail when guys from our wrestling team beat the shit out of a rival team before a meet and Joey had a baseball bat. "Boys will be boys."

Anyway. I can see this other guy. Guy I had to practice with. But can't recall his name. It might have been "Jeff." He was mean. He was Varsity, and I was Junior Varsity. After practice, he would pee on your leg in the communal showers. To show his dominance.

I remember thinking how lamely transparent that was. Lights went on in darkened and unexplored rooms of my mind. There are people who need to humiliate other people. I was afraid of him but suddenly aware of his limitations. I had not understood before this the potency of the cards I was holding. My need to strike back and the willingness to do so.

I don't want to be defined by humiliation.

Anyway. This guy I wrestled with. He wrestled mean. In practice. Nobody wanted to practice with him. There was an unwritten rule: in practice with your teammates, you didn't fight dirty. We all knew ways to turn a block into a hidden punch. Hell, the coach taught us how to hide a dirty wrist bone to the jaw. Unwritten rule. You didn't do that shit to your teammates, only guys from the other team.

Anyway. This guy I used to wrestle in practice was mean. I spent my entire sophomore year with a black eye. Hit someone in the nose hard enough, and their eye turns green and purple and black. He beat the shit out of me, and I was afraid of him.

But like I said, I knew I was smarter than him. I knew I had the meanness and, at the same time, more colors on my pallet. Still, he scared me. Made me see my own cowardice.

And I don't believe, even to this day, I have entirely forgiven him for that.

Anyway. In the dullness of a Michigan winter. One afternoon. After school. When the shadows grew long and you knew you had to wait in the dark and the snot-freezing cold to be picked up by your Dad after practice. (I feel the rush now that accompanied the hope, and then the fear, the fear of disappointment, and then the recognition, the recognition and joy of familiar headlights on a dark road. My Dad!) Anyway, one day in practice this guy. This Varsity guy. 98 pounds. With pubic hair and everything. Was really giving me the business. He was hitting me hard. Not like all in good fun, you understand, but like he wanted to hurt me. I had reached my limit, my breaking point. I was afraid of him. He hit me one too many times, and I broke his nose.

In half-sobs, he turned to my fellow Junior Varsity lightweights. This guy. He was Varsity, you understand. And he was fighting back the tears and bleeding profusely. Bleating like a lamb. Just another sacrifice. And I was Junior Varsity. And he turned to my people, my fellow Junior Varsity lightweights, blinking back the tears.

And he said to them. This is what he said: "This is what I'm talking about, Pilgrim is the only one of you who has the guts to wrestle."

His bravado fell short. Hollow. The coward in the bully revealed. And I saw my comrades shrink back from him in contempt and look at me in admiration. I was so proud. He never peed on my leg again.

Anyway. What I remember most is the disgust I felt having wasted so much fear on someone who turned out to be so weak. Even weaker than me. I felt contempt for him. I enjoyed the contempt. And then I felt sick. And felt contempt for myself. All the sorrow and rage.

I quit the wrestling team after that year. I became someone else.

Still, sometimes I remember that punch I threw that broke his nose. I remember how good it felt. The memory is tinged with both shame and pride. Never to be resolved. In *The Night of the Hunter*, there is "L-O-V-E" tattooed on one fist, and "H-A-T-E" on the other. Robert Mitchum. Leaning on the everlasting arms.

Anyway. This memory. This memory of rage and sorrow and blood. This memory tinged with shame and pride. It stands outside the law. I always have one foot in that place. Outside the law.

But just one.

I was walking down the Plymouth Road, and my right hand didn't know what my left was doing. My left hand was shaking in fury, and my right hand was reaching out. Seeking hands to hold. Not wanting to be alone.

"You damn fool!" the Rabbi hooted. "You're going to get us killed!"

I hit him as hard as I could with my left hand.

"Got that out of your system?" he asked.

I reached in love for his hand with my right.

"You done now?" he asked.

"It's both/and," he said. "Not either/or. Got it? Both/and, not either/or."

I wanted to crucify him. I wanted to kiss him.

And his eyes flashed. Nothing but the facts, ma'am. And in the flashing was reflection. I saw myself. And slipped out of my skin and walked between my left hand and my right. Free. Through the great refusal.

And I walked. One foot in front of the other. Grace made concrete. Arms a-swinging back and forth. Not either/or. I walked. Between my left hand and my right. Both/and. Through the great refusal.

Just like a saint. Just like a sinner. Simultaneously.

And I walked. All punch-drunk and justified.

Series Four

I was walking down the Plymouth Road with the Rabbi, and we came upon the Devil. He was standing on the side of the road, and he couldn't catch his breath. He was doubled over, coughing up a lung. He had made his bed, and now he was being asked to lie in it.

He gasped and he gasped.

"You are so weak," I said. I was enjoying my advantage.

"Mercy!" he cried, convulsing and gasping.

If the Devil asks for mercy, can you trust him? When you're not looking, when you begin to believe that the coast is clear, that you can relax your grip, isn't that when the Devil plunges the shank between beautifully articulated ribs?

I panicked. I collapsed in a fit of coughing. Bent over on the side of the road. Couldn't catch my breath. Me and the Devil on the side of the road. Hacking up our lungs.

There was willfulness that connected us. There was a willfulness.

"It's what drew me to you," the Devil said.

"But you made the will something ugly. You reduced it."

"The will? It's what drew you to me," the Devil said.

He was telling the truth. And that sucked.

"We're not so different," he said.

"No. We're not."

I looked at my soul, and it was a microcosm. The world in a snowflake. It was a frozen wasteland. Cold crystal. Speechless. Frozen but heating up. The great refusal. I looked at my soul, and it was the great break-up of language, the crack-up in which Hayim Bialik, poet of the valley of the dry bones, poet without language—(Can these dry bones live? Can life be breathed into this dead language?)—leapt from ice floe to ice floe. The break-up of language. Pursuing the Name of God. The Name of God. Ever receding. Ever demanding. Dr. Frankenstein pursuing his creature. From ice floe to ice floe. Leaping. Melting. Word to word. Image to image. Metaphor to metaphor. The Name of God. Grasshoppers. Fugitives on the run. Hope to hope. Golems walking on ice. Completing the sentence. Melting ice. And not the thought. Walking on water. Melting words. Always falling short of uttering the Name of God. In the Holy Silence. As the expanse of frigid water grows, separating ice floe from ice floe. Opening the breach. Global warming. In the climate of the soul.

"Just say it," the Devil said. "Say the Name of God!"

"It's forbidden."

The Devil looked at me. He was so effing lonely. He looked at me.

I met his stare with my own. I gave him the look. I channeled Jimmy Cagney. "Whaddaya say? Whaddaya know?" I gave him Humphrey Bogart eyes.

But the Devil looked me in my own eye.

"Say the Name of God. Just do it! Do what is forbidden!"

I reached for someone else's eyes and got nothing. I had nothing left but my own eyes. My own gaze. I looked at the Devil with my own eyes. I looked the Devil in the eye. And I said, me and Bartleby the Scrivener, this is what I said, "I'd prefer not to."

"You weren't ever going to have the guts," the Devil exploded, his eyes bulging and his words sputtering. "You never had what it takes!"

I choked on my "No," and I panicked and hunched over on the side of the road. Couldn't catch my breath. Choking on my "Yes." The Plymouth Road. And liked to cough up a lung. Couldn't catch my breath. I gasped and gasped.

Weak. And naked. And broken.

And in the silence. And in the great refusal. The Rabbi stepped forward. And created a space in his stepping forward. *Tzimtzum.* And he pronounced the Name of God. The holy Name of God. *Ein Sof.* The sacred Name that must not be uttered. *Ha Shem.* Tetragrammaton. *Yud. Hey. Vav. Hey.*

He did what is forbidden.

And nothing happened. And no one stoned him. We had already crucified him; we have *always* crucified him. And the world was not destroyed. And everybody had to learn to live with having heard the Name of God uttered. Learn to live with the fact that what had been forbidden had been done. All-ye, all-ye, in come free! And how it had changed nothing.

And in the confusion, I reached for the Devil and gently grasped his neck and drew him close and kissed him full on the mouth.

And I knew healing. And St. Francis' leper. And the creation of a New Heaven and a New Earth. In the Yes and No of my salvation. In my dialectic. *Todo y Nada.* And how it changed everything.

And nothing.

And everything.

And nothing....
And everything....
And....

I fell down at the feet of the Rabbi, and he said, "Get up," and he let his eyes linger on mine, and, in his eyes, I saw God and the Devil, and I saw myself, and I saw the Rabbi. And I saw my brother. And I saw my sister. The whole world in his eyes. And the Rabbi said, this is what he said, with impatience, "Get up!"

Talitha cumi.

And so I got up. And we just kept walking.

I was walking down the Plymouth Road with the Rabbi, and we were not alone. We were walking with the Man of Constant Sorrow and the Man of Constant Rage. And I did not know how we had come to be in their company.

And so I turned to the Rabbi, and I asked him. Asked how we had come to be in the company of the Man of Constant Sorrow and the Man of Constant Rage.

And the Rabbi lifted his right hand and with the wave of his cloak, I saw Raskolnikov from *Crime and Punishment*. He was dreaming. They were beating a horse. It was brutal.

And the Rabbi lifted his left hand and with the wave of his cloak, I saw Friedrich Nietzsche. He was insane. The people were beating a horse. It was brutal.

"Very funny," I said. "But why are they here?"

"They are always here."

"I know. But why are they here now?"

"Because they are always here."

I let that ride for a while. Let it sink in.

And then after a while, he said, "Because you keep beating the horse."

Somewhere, someone pinned a butterfly in a collection.

I stood convicted, and the road held my weight.

"Well, if they're going to walk with us," I said, "we better get to know their names."

The Man of Constant Sorrow turned to me and said, "You can call me 'Vincent.'"

The Man of Constant Rage turned to me and said, "Yeah, that works. You can call me 'Vincent,' too."

Once, when I was in New York, they had van Gogh's *Wheat Field with Crows* at MoMA. You felt the painting before you entered the room. And once you did—enter the room—the painting commanded all attention. It throbbed in person in a way it didn't in reproductions. Sucked all the oxygen out of the room. I couldn't breathe.

It was the Word of God. And it was blasphemy. Both/and.

On the Plymouth Road, suddenly Picasso's *Guernica* rose up and pierced me.

I gave the Rabbi the look.

He gave it right back.

"I know what you're doing," I said.

"I know you do," he replied. "Can you maybe just this once listen?"

"I suppose," I replied.

"Quit beating the horse," he said. "It's not her fault."

Something broke in me on the Plymouth Road. The road I had taken as an alternative to every Main Street I had inherited.

I didn't want to beat the horse anymore. I just didn't know how to stop.

I was walking down the Plymouth Road with the Rabbi, and I came upon the Keening Mother. She had lost her children like Rachel, and she was inconsolable. *For they were no more.* Her sharpest blows shattered the air, and her pleas for mercy muddied the waters.

She raged. She mourned. But she could not find her way back. She was lost in the howling.

I stopped on the Plymouth Road. Me and the Rabbi. And I tried to console the Keening Mother. But all she could see in me was her loss and her rage. I felt the ground shift beneath my feet. And I felt the power of the undertow. Sucked in. Ground up. Fuel for the rage.

Rip current.

I did not want to end it that way. I did not want to be a bit player in someone else's movie. An extra. Swallowed.

I wanted to live. And could no longer pay her price.

"So what are you going to do about the Keening Mother?" the Rabbi asked.

"I don't like your tone," I said.

"You don't like my tone?"

"Yeah. Tone."

"So you want I should maybe soften it?"

"Well, I mean...would it kill you to maybe show a little love?"

"Oh, and if I showed you a little love, you could accept it?"

"You're such a jerk."

"She can't let go," the Rabbi said.

"Not my problem," I said.

"So who needs to show a little love now?"

"Jesus Christ! You're such an asshole!"

"Language, Pilgrim," he said, "language." But his tone was not a provocation. There was a sadness in it. The sadness of the Garden. So alone in Gethsemane.

"She's like fucking Kryptonite," I pleaded.

"You're not Superman."

"No shit, Sherlock!"

"She's lost," the Rabbi said.

"So am I!"

The love between us just hung heavy in the air.

All that love. It was suffocating me. It was killing me. It was egging me on, provoking me, agitating me, disrupting me, unfolding me. I was being swallowed.

The Keening Mother stood in the middle of the Plymouth Road and took a spade to it. Tried to dig it under. It was silly and futile.

She was old and frail and a little pathetic. Her sorrow had gone to seed. Her rage was toxic.

The Rabbi looked at me.

I hauled away the dirt she excavated from the Plymouth Road. The Keening Mother. I got a wheelbarrow and just carted it away.

"I'm not going to be a patsy!" I screamed at the Rabbi.

"You want a hand with that load?" he asked, tilting his head toward the wheelbarrow.

"I can't do this." I said in all candor.

"I know," he said. "Do it anyway."

"I'm never going to get there," I said.

"You've never left there," he said.

Love hung heavy in the air.

I was walking down the Plymouth Road with the Rabbi, and we were not alone. We were walking with Rebbe Menachem Mendel, the Kotzker. One Sabbath eve, the Kotzker emerged from his study, approached the front of the synagogue, and blew out the Sabbath candles. He flung his *kiddush* cup to the ground. He removed his *yarmulke* and declared that "there is neither justice nor judge." He turned and left his people alone in the dark on the Sabbath.

They kept faith for nineteen years until he died. The Kotzker left his room only once a year for *Bedikah Chametz*. His people kept faith until one by one they drifted off to other Rebbes.

"This is Rebbe Menachem," the Rabbi said.

"Good to meet you."

He didn't reply.

"He's kind of shy," the Rabbi said.

We just kept walking.

Our new companion made me uncomfortable. His silence was oppressive. Time was sodden.

We walked a while in unease.

"He doesn't want anything from you," the Rabbi said.

I looked at Menachem, and he looked at me.

We just walked a while. Keeping company.

Once, when I was young, someone I cared about traveled to Assisi and came back to me with a St. Francis medal. It was blessed by the Pope. JP II. I treasured it. (Hadn't Francis himself appeared to me in dreams when I was trying to make up my mind, one way or the other, to enter the Ministry?) Later, when I was not quite so young, someone else, who had demanded it of me as proof of my devotion, threw it out the window of a car on Lake Shore Drive in Chicago in a moment of pique.

Without thinking, without thought, I struck out and hit her. Blew out the Sabbath candles.

We just walked in silence. I, the Rabbi, and the Kotzker. Had nothing to say.

The sharp smell of extinguished candles was violent in the air and in our noses. It just costs so much to say. It just costs so much to *be*.

"If you meet the Buddha on the road," the Rabbi said, a twinkle in his eye, "slay him."

No one laughed. It wasn't funny.

"About noon the next day, as they were on their journey and approaching the city, Peter went up on the roof to pray. He became hungry and wanted something to eat; and while it was being prepared, he fell into a trance. He saw the heaven opened and something like a large sheet coming down, being lowered to the ground by its four corners. In it were all kinds of four-footed creatures and reptiles and birds of the air. Then he heard a voice saying, 'Get up, Peter; kill and eat.' But Peter said, 'By no means, Lord; for I have never eaten anything that is profane or unclean.' The voice said to him again, a second time, 'What God has made clean, you must not call profane.' This happened three times, and the thing was suddenly taken up to heaven."

Acts 10:9-19

We were walking down the Plymouth Road, the Rabbi and I, and we came upon the Pearl of Great Price. We're talking the Holy Grail here. The thing of value for which you give everything. And it was disgusting.

I mean, it was right there, in the middle of the Plymouth Road, the Pearl of Great Price, stopping traffic, and it was effing vile. There was retching and gagging. But the ugly thing was still just there. In the middle of the Road. And it filled us with revulsion.

"Okay. Now what?" I asked the Rabbi.

"It's your call, Pilgrim."

"This is a test, isn't it?"

"Why are you so obsessed with tests? Everything is a test with you!"

"Everything's a test with *you*!" I said with too much heat.

"I know you are, but what am I?"

He was baiting me. Trying to get my goat.

"That thing's effing disgusting!"

"It's the Pearl of Great Price. Can you swallow it?"

"I'm sorry," I said with as much shade as possible, "you want me to swallow it?"

"Yes," he said, refusing to react to my shade—much to my annoyance.

"Don't that just beat all?" I screamed, trying to nail him to the wall.

"It's the Pearl of Great Price," he said with unnerving calm. "What are you going to do?"

Then, the Rabbi took off his mask and winked at me. Very theatrically.

"It can't be swallowed, can it?" I asked.

"Nope."

"You're a real jerk, you know that?"

"I've been told."

"It's going to swallow *me*, isn't it?" I asked.

"Already has," he said.

"It's the Pearl of Great Price," I said.

"This is what I'm saying," he said.

"What the hey? Bring it on."

I swallowed the Pearl of Great Price and was swallowed.

"This is my body," he said.

"Very funny," I replied.

"Broken for you."

"Still not funny," I said.

And then we laughed.

After having left—and then returned—to the Plymouth Road, it was not a surprise that the Road I had returned to was not the Road I had left. The Road had become more personal, at the exact point where what had been confined to the personal was becoming more public.

Which is to say, the Plymouth Road, after I had returned, was full of fellow travelers, who came from alien imaginations. Strangers from a strange land with strange ideas of home. Diversity is a bitch.

The Road was clogged with seekers and pilgrims. Refugees and immigrants. And some of them were, quite frankly, toxic and dangerous. Love fought it out with hate. And everyone had a concealed weapon permit on the Plymouth Road.

How strange to share your pilgrimage with souls who either didn't want to get to where you thought and hoped and prayed you were going or, more disturbingly, didn't want to get where you wanted to get at all but, indeed, envisioned a different city on a hill, a city you could not inhabit, in which you could breath, or move, or have your being.

Because hate is toxic. And was no home at all.

But they were on the Road. And they were pilgrims. Just like you.

There was a circle to be squared. An eye of the needle to be threaded.

How can you love what wants to destroy love? And how can you love when that thing that wants to destroy love is in you? I mean. We were on the same. Effing. Road. The Plymouth Road. The cold, hard mirror. The humiliating promise of something more.

Through a glass darkly.

It was a confusing time on the Plymouth Road. Pilgrims hung on by the skin of their teeth. Hate made its case. Love was mocked and jeered in courtyards and circular drives. The hate in us warred with the love in us. The personal was public. The public was personal.

One step was love. The next was hate. And yet, so much depended upon a red wheelbarrow. So much depended upon each and every pilgrim on the Plymouth Road. And we just kept walking. One step. And then another. One step. And then another.

But we walked on the Plymouth Road. Each and every one of us. And we just kept walking. And some of us walked and climbed. Jacob's Ladder. Some of us walked and climbed. But none of us knew which ones were actually climbing. In fact, all of us thought we were the ones climbing. And were sure that the others weren't. Jacob's Ladder. But not all of us were.

Climbing.

Or maybe none of us were.

Or all of us.

But we walked.

Each and every one of us afraid of the thing that walked in us.

The thing that walked in us.

The Rabbi proved to be a real mensch. He did not lie about the cost. But he demanded. He asserted. He revealed. That the light shines in the darkness and was not overcome. And I believed him.

I was walking down the Plymouth Road with the Rabbi, and we were tired, and the ground opened up beneath us until we each had to leap to our own side. The opening became a fissure on the Plymouth Road, and my real life presented itself. Structural problems. I couldn't be here and there at the same time. I was a man with responsibilities. I carried a rickety structure on my back in the shape of a steeple, in Lansing, with my wife, as the fissure widened, and I saw the Rabbi fade away, and he was on his side and I was on my own. My real life. With all my responsibilities. With my wife. And everyone I loved and held dear and felt responsible for. My stepson. A rickety structure always threatening to collapse. And the Rabbi just receded.

There was a moment. A clearing in time. A choice. I could panic. Like I always had. I could replay the scene. Endlessly. I could lose myself in the loop. Or I could just wait it out. Let the moment be what it was. A photograph ripped from the movie. Let it play itself out. Rip the moment from time. Stay firm. Eyes on the prize. Let it go. I seized the moment.

And released it.

When the fissure closed up as consequence, and the Rabbi came back, he looked pleased with me. He didn't say anything. I carried my steeple on my back, my rickety structure, my real life, on the Plymouth Road. Just like my father, carrying a country on his back. Sisyphus. The Rabbi pretended he didn't notice.

But I saw his smile. That's the thing about the Rabbi. He always made sure you saw his smile.

"You hungry?" he asked.

"I could eat."

"Mexican?" he asked.
"El Oasis Taco Truck?"
"On Michigan Ave.?"
"Sounds good," I said.
"They have Mexican Coke. Real cane sugar."
"You paying?"
"Always," he said.
Smiling.

> "The breeze blew from the turret
> As I parted his locks;
> With his gentle hand
> He wounded my neck
> And caused all my senses to be suspended.
> I remained, lost in oblivion;
> My face I reclined on the Beloved.
> All ceased and I abandoned myself,
> Leaving my cares
> forgotten among the lilies."
> —St. John of the Cross, "On a Dark Night"

I want to post here each and every lyric of Kris Kristofferson's song, "To Beat the Devil." I want to post it so bad.

"The way upward and the way downward is one and the same."
—Heraclitus

I was walking down the Plymouth Road with the Rabbi, and I was tired. Dead-dried-desiccated-bone tired. Heavy. I was so tired and so heavy that the Road would not hold my weight. Gravity would not cooperate. I raised and cupped my hands like a diver—I knew I was going somewhere—but instead of ascending, I descended. Bottom dropped out. I just dropped.

And as I fell, I accelerated. And as I accelerated, I began to heat up. And pretty soon, there were flames. And I blazed. As I plummeted, as I fell, as I dropped. I blazed.

Something about friction.

Everything I've ever read that stuck with me, every image that stopped the works like a wrench in the gears, every hook from every pop song, every kindness that ever terrified me, every weirdo and every dork, every landing stuck, every kiss, every charming turn of the wrist, every single one of Vincent van Gogh's holy shoes, every moment of Grace, every God-swallowed moment in my falling life, my plummeting life, my enflamed, my entorched, my descending life, swaddled me and scorched me and reduced me to cinders.

I just kept falling, and there was no end to the falling until the falling itself just became the environment in which you lived and moved and had your being. Until the reduction itself, the very cinder-ness of it all, became just the next thing from which you're going to be reduced, one more stop on the eternal underground railroad.

And so the falling itself ceased to be falling. And in fact, it became ascending. Or might as well have been. Ascending? Descending? It was just the space in which you made your peace with time and raised your children and loved your wife and tried to do something good.

One more light of the world.

"Looking good, Pilgrim!" the Rabbi said.

"Feeling good, Rabbi!" I said.

Thumbs ups all around.

"I'm not going to feel my tiredness like this all the time, am I?" I asked the Rabbi.

"Nope."

"Might as well enjoy it."

"That would be my advice," the Rabbi said.

We didn't laugh because we didn't have to. There is something deeper than laughter. Don't get me wrong. It's still funny. It's just deeper than laughter. Deeper than tears.

The other side of reduction is expansion. You exhale. You inhale. You exhale. You inhale. You kiss the Devil.

"Hey Pilgrim," the Rabbi said, "you hear about the guy who said he bit himself on the forehead?"

"Yeah."

"He stood on a chair."

"That's not funny."

"Yes it is."

"Okay. You're right. It's kind of funny."

SERIES FIVE
BLOOD OF CHRIST

Do not think that I have come to bring peace to the
earth; I have not come to bring peace, but a sword.
Matthew 10:34

But when the disciples saw him walking on the sea, they
were terrified, saying, "It is a ghost!" And they cried out
in fear. But immediately Jesus spoke to them and said,
"Take heart, it is I; do not be afraid." Peter answered
him, "Lord, if it is you, command me to come to you on
the water." He said, "Come." So Peter got out of the
boat, started walking on the water, and came toward
Jesus. But when he noticed the strong wind, he became
frightened, and beginning to sink, he cried out, "Lord,
save me!"
Matthew 14:26-30

Reciprocity
9/11/16

I was walking with the Rabbi down the Plymouth Road. And a city main broke, and the water burst like a bubble, and flooded the road with nonstop flow and pressure and catastrophe. Like an open artery. The sheer force. And good and bad pilgrims alike were washed away in the flow. On the Plymouth Road.

Fast forward, fifteen years later. And you can still feel the pressure, the force of the wind, the heroic leaning in, long after it has all subsided. Like a ghost.

Fast forward, fifteen years later.

9/11.

These days it's just something you don't want to talk about anymore.

Thar she blows!

The ship left port.

"And I alone survived to...."

It was fifteen years later, and I was surprised by the emotions that hit me. Walking on the Plymouth Road. Ambushed by feelings and ambiguities. The first responders. The workers at Ground Zero. Lung disease. Respiratory ailments. The smell, like burning tires, that permeated everything. The reek of bombs.

I was walking down the Plymouth Road with the Rabbi, and it was flooded, and every subtlety was elided and erased, and there just wasn't anything more than what it was.

Over 91,000 Afghani souls.

174,000 Iraqi souls.

All those souls.

And the 6,800 souls of Americans.

All that blood.

And the American soul.

I was naked, and the Rabbi wasn't wearing any mask.

I looked at him, and, in the twinkle of his eye, I saw....

"Are you okay?" I asked the Rabbi.

He looked at me with a look of perfect terror. "What do you mean?" he asked.

"You look swallowed."

"Swallowed?"

"Yeah. Swallowed."

He looked me in the eye.

It can't be easy being the Rabbi. All so human.

The Rabbi leaned in to me. Crumpled in my arms. There was just so much. And so much. So much. And accepted my warmth. And I just held him. We held on to each other.

I held the Rabbi. And he held me.

Fast forward, fifteen years later. And the hand that was being touched could not differentiate itself from the hand that was touching.

Fast forward, fifteen years later. My heart broke. And against my will, love abounded. All so divine.

The Rabbi accepted my love.

As the blood coursed through our veins. And dripped from five holy wounds.

Grand Guignol:
The Twins

I was dreaming. And in this dream, I was Abel. And I was watching my brother, Cain. And he was chopping with an ax at the roots of a great tree. Tree of Life. But he was standing in a swamp. This is Cain we're talking about here. He was sluicing about the swamp. And there was no purchase. And he was slipping and sinking. And he was chopping at his own legs. His limbs. And there was just no difference between roots and branches. Or legs and arms.

Some things grow upward, and some things grow down.

My brother, Cain, stopped and gave a rebel yell. He held the ax in one hand and let the other wave free, like the swell of a chorus, and his slowly extended finger left a slow motion trail of blood. And we were lost in the mist. The wind-blown, bloody mist. And we were sinking in the swamp.

And I was watching my brother, Cain. And I was not able to wake up. And he hadn't even murdered me yet.

I was lost in the mist and going down. Chopping at my own legs. Tree of Life. Trying to suss out my own responsibility. Before it was too late.

I was lost and couldn't wake up. Just like Cain.

With my face so blood-mist-stippled.

Plymouth Road Memoir:
Diving for Pearls

When I was young, I dived deep for pearls. I wonder now, that I am not young, if I am not experiencing the bends.

Where I was once fearless, lithe, strong, and clueless, I am now fearful, rude, compromised, and informed. A little bit of knowledge is a dangerous thing. Every time you play out more string for the kite in the wind, you slacken the muscles to draw it back in. If you're not careful, that string is going to snap. It's going to go beyond your control. You're not going to be able to reel it back in. We weaken with every resistance overcome. It just takes a while to feel it in your bones, your muscles, your body that keeps betraying you.

There is the fact of the wind. *Ruach. Pneuma.* Holy Spirit. And the fact that our skin is only so elastic and can bear the wind only so much, before we must shatter and founder and fold and fall from the sky to the earth.

And then you discover the string that can't be snapped. And the kite that does not fold. And the flight without end.

And then you discover the snapping of the string and the crashing of the kite, and the flight that ends.

And there is no difference between that, and the string that cannot be snapped, and the kite that does not fold, and the flight without end.

And you just stand there.

Only just now, beginning to realize, that you are standing. Like Peter on the water. Standing on the water. Just seconds before the fear that will make you sink.

The Man Who Wasn't Yukio Mishima

I was walking down the Plymouth Road. It was me and the Rabbi. And we came upon a man sitting in a meadow. And he looked a lot like Yukio Mishima. On his forehead, he wore a scarlet kerchief, and on that kerchief were words in white, in a language I did not read. And he had a pistol to his temple. And he sat in the meadow, as still as "a speeding locomotive abandoned for years to the delirium of a virgin forest." Full of mad love. He pulled the pistol from his temple and spun the chamber. He returned the pistol to his temple. He shouted, "Purgation! *Hai!*" counted his breaths and pulled the trigger.

Nothing happened.

He pulled the pistol from his temple again and spun the chamber. He returned the pistol to his temple. He shouted, "Illumination! *Hai!*" counted his breaths and pulled the trigger.

Nothing happened.

Finally, he pulled the pistol from his temple one last time and spun the chamber. He returned the pistol to his temple. He shouted, "Union! *Hai!*" counted his breaths and pulled the trigger.

The meadow grass waved in the wind so much like reeds in shallow lakes in the Midwest, that the meadow itself, became a lake. The man stood up. Turned. And looked at me. He'd blown off half his face. Drip, drip, drip. Into the lake. He just looked at me.

Every golden pavilion, every lovely thing, every chorus of every radio song, every inside joke, every spontaneous joining of hands in the face of awe, every secret coronation among the freaks and the creeps and the dorks, the vindication of the blind and the deaf, the rhythm of the halt, the joy of captives released, and the day of the LORD, every little letter from home, just dripped into the lake. Drip, drip, drip.

I looked closer, and it wasn't Yukio Mishima. It was someone else. Looking at me. Dripping into the lake.

I turned to the Rabbi. "Nice," I said, "and it's not even Halloween."

And out of the bloodied, open mouth of the man who was not Yukio Mishima, entire souls and persons and individuals began to climb out, like passengers manning the lifeboats, and they just stood there, looking stunned, blinking in the sun, in the meadow, that had become a lake. There were tons of them. The people who came from the blood-clotted mouth of the man in the meadow. They just kept coming from the open mouth of the man who was not Yukio Mishima.

I looked at the Rabbi.

"You don't have to kill yourself, Pilgrim," he said.

"I know. I just have to be born."

"Birth is violent," he said.

"Tell me about it."

I just stood there and stared at the people who had climbed out of the mouth of the man who was not Yukio Mishima. And they just stared right back at me.

"Everything that is necessary has been given. You could breathe."

Drip. Drip. Drip. Into the lake.

"You could live."

"In the beginning when God created the heavens and
the earth, the earth was a formless void and darkness
covered the face of the deep, while a wind from God
swept over the face of the waters."

Genesis 1:1-2

Black Lives Matter

To speak the truth is one thing; to let it be true is another. Gospel truth. Pilgrim had spoken the truth every day of his ordained life, Gospel truth, but he had only let it be true for him, himself, in moments discrete. It hurts to be loved.

And it's not as if it's easy to let truth be true in the first place. There are a lot of factors to be considered. We have responsibilities beyond ourselves. And the whole thing is kind of slippery. It hurts to love.

Truth has consequences, and, where there are consequences, someone is going to get hurt.

It's a world of hurt out there, my brothers and sisters. Because if you are going to truck with truth, if you are going to traffic in such goods, you are going to hurt. You are going to hurt others. You are going to get hurt. There's just no way around it. It just hurts.

And it's not as if the alternative is any better. To not speak the truth, Gospel truth, is pretty much to guarantee more hurting, both to the one who speaks and to the one to whom one speaks. The violence of not speaking the truth. Gospel truth. But this kind of hurting, this kind of violence, is stupid hurting. The kind of indiscriminate hurting in which all are brought low. And healing itself is swallowed and absorbed in the inevitability of hurting. Everything hurts. Everything hurts. Still. There is healing. And stupid hurting wants to avoid it. Avoid the hurting. Avoid the healing.

Because it hurts to heal. Because it hurts. Because it fucking hurts.

Pilgrim was looking for the smart hurting. Always calculating the angles. But he just wasn't that smart. And it just fucking hurt.

It was no skin off the Rabbi's nose. He was going to be there either way. Making the hurt pay. Whether Pilgrim liked it or not.

Because that's what he does. The Rabbi.

Make the hurting pay.

Make the dirt stick.

I was walking down the Plymouth Road with the Rabbi but was in a boat on the water, and it was night, and we had no lantern. Out of the mist and through the darkness, the light coming from some unknown source, a figure came steadily walking toward us. And I totally freaked.

The waves lapped at the boat like hands slapping faces, and that thing just kept walking, just kept walking toward us, on the water. And I freaked.

I begged it not to come any closer. That thing! That abomination!

I turned to the Rabbi and screamed, "What should we do?"

And a voice said, "What do you mean 'we,' kemosabe"?

And I said, because I couldn't help myself, "That's not funny anymore."

And he said, "Yes, it is."

"Kind of getting old, if you know what I mean."

And it was only then that I realized that the Rabbi wasn't there with me in the boat.

And that thing just kept walking. Walking on the water. Like the Fear of the LORD. Which is the beginning of wisdom.

But not the end.

And I panicked. And I begged it not to come any closer. And it just kept coming closer. And it was like one of those dreams where you try to run and can't move your legs.

And then it stopped. That thing. Walking out of the dark and into the light, on the water.

And it said, "Okay, I'll make a deal with you."

"A deal?"

Someone turned on the electric lights, and I started to see some angles.

"Yeah. A deal."

"Okay. Shoot."

"I won't come any closer if you get out of the boat and come closer to me."

"Let me get this straight."

"Go on, I'm with you."

"You won't come any closer, if I get out of the boat and come closer to you?"

"Yeah. That's the long and short of it."

"So, what you're saying is that if I get out of *this* boat, walk on *that* water, and come closer to *you*, you won't come any closer to me?"

"That's what I'm saying."

"What do you think, Rabbi?" I asked.

But he wasn't in the boat.

I looked at the thing on the water and asked, "What's in it for me?"

"Well, it would stop the immediate panic."

"Stop the immediate panic."

"That's what I said."

"And you think that's worth something?"

"Don't you?"

I thought a moment and then said, "Yeah."

I was already out of the boat and three steps toward the thing when I realized that I was walking on water. I started to sink.

And found myself in the Rabbi's arms.

On the side of the Road. With no boat. And no water. And the Plymouth Road holding my weight.

"I've got to say," I whispered in his ear, "the production values on this one were really state of the art."

"No expense spared, Pilgrim."

"I appreciate the little touches."

"Don't mention it."

We let go of each other and walked down the Plymouth Road.

In noncontiguous yet discrete moments, the fear sputtered and disappeared. For entire moments. As the subtle vibrations of the mansion on the hill began to reveal themselves like light trapped in trees.

A Plymouth Road
Interlude

Vigil: Interrupted

And then my wife, my baby, died....

I was walking down the Plymouth Road with the Rabbi, and we came upon the disciples who had just handed over their master to the authorities. They had each kissed him once on the cheek and handed him over.

Their hands waved in weird-palm hosannas like the seaweed undulating in time in that old Robert Mitchum movie *The Night of the Hunter*, undulating, when the drunken ferryman saw the murdered woman in her car at the bottom of the river, Shelley Winters, and her hair was caught in the current. All the hands were waving. All the arms were undulating. As they handed over their master to the authorities. Like seaweed and hair.

The Birth of Venus.

I had handed over my Mary. My wife. Handed over my Ms. Mary to the authorities. To the specialists. To the illness. To the inevitability. Handed her over. To the tubes and the staples and the holes in her belly, and the surgeons and the punctures and the bruises, and the weeping of arms and the violence of the sucking of the phlegm from lungs, the sucking of phlegm from pneumonia-clogged air sacs. I had handed over my beloved.

Septic.

Ever since it had become clear that Ms. Mary might actually die, and, now that's she gone, I've had the unsettling feeling that there're only three walls left, or maybe, that the front door has been left open. I feel exposed. I didn't expect that.

What also surprised me throughout the whole deal was the urgent need to see the movie *Papillon* again. Do you guys remember that movie? Steve McQueen and Dustin Hoffman. I watched it with Mary's best friend, Karen, and Elias, my stepson, the night before Elias left to go back to Boston. The night after his mother had died. It was his first time seeing it, and he was blown away. Loved it. We both seemed to recognize something about ourselves and our new situation in that movie.

I was walking down the Plymouth Road with the Rabbi, and we came upon the disciples. Their hands empty and reaching and grasping and hungry for what they had always and already handed over. They stood stupid with their shattered and stunned faces.

And I saw Abraham and his bound son, Isaac. And I saw him hand over his son. This is Abraham we're talking about here. Like in the Bible. Just handed him over. Handed over the Promise. Handed over the *fulfillment* of the Promise. Handed over Isaac, which means "laughter" in Hebrew. Abraham just handed over laughter.

In fear and trembling.

In plain English.

And I turned to the Rabbi.

And he was nowhere to be found. And he was everywhere. In the pus and the piss and the bile and the blood.

And I let her go. I let her go. I let my baby go.

"Is this what is required?" I asked. "Do you have to give it away to get it back?"

Ms. Mary passed away today at 1:53 PM. In the last couple of days, she had become conscious enough to tell us what her wishes were concerning further treatment. It was a gift. A grace. She fought her way out of God knows what kind of fog and whirlwind-whipped half-light so that we would know that we were loved. That we had mattered. That she wanted to go home. Wanted to see her mother and her father and her sister. Wanted to let go. Wanted to sink deep, deep into that black water, in the deepest and darkest of wells, where she could sleep and dream forever in the light. She was fifty-five years old.

And she came back! My baby came back! And Jesus came back. But he couldn't stick around. He just came back for a quick buss on the cheek and then was gone again. Ascended on high. Sitting at the right hand of God the Father Almighty. Or wherever. And she came back. She came back.

And I said, are you going to stay?

And she said, if you want me to, *Yeah!*

But that was just a line in a Bob Dylan song.

And I said, are you going to stay?

But she didn't say a damned thing. Her hair just waved like seaweed in a movie or a myth. And she didn't say a damned thing. And the Rabbi didn't say a damned thing. And then she said. This is what she said: "No."

In particular, I wanted to rewatch a scene I remembered from *Papillon* where prisoners in solitary confinement stick their heads out of holes in their prison doors, while prison officials check for lice. The prisoners look at each other. They ask each other how they look.

The first time it happens, Steve McQueen is indifferent when an older man asks him.

"Fine," he says, almost impatiently.

Later, after his hair has turned white and he himself has aged deeply, he echoes the old man's question, and a younger man reacts much as Steve McQueen had reacted the first time.

That scene kept recurring to me.

Strange. Feeling exposed and wanting to hide—and then feeling the need to be seen, to be recognized in order to recognize yourself—simultaneously.

It feels like I'm going to have to get used to myself all over again without Ms. Mary. This seems preposterous to me. I haven't been myself without Ms. Mary for so long that I'm not quite certain how to be at all.

I'm kind of curious. I mean, beyond the bracing for those sudden and searing stabs of loss and grief. Behind it is a new curiosity.

And then my baby died....

I was walking down the Plymouth Road. No. I was not walking. I was not fucking walking. Fuck the Plymouth Road! I was keening. I was twirling. Slowly at first. And I was rising. Arms extended. I was slowly rising. My feet were bare. I was twirling. Arms extended. I had lost my red shoes. And I was not touching the road. I was fucking twirling. Weathervane caught in the storm. Arms extended.

And I was engulfed in flames. Flames of grief. I was slowly rising. Flames licking limbs. Flames of violence. Flames of rage. And then I was spinning faster. And I was rising faster. And the flames were rising like shrieks. Flames of sorrow. Flames of terror. Arms extended. And parts of me were splitting into sparks. And the sparks were rising and glowing and then fading. And I was just never going to get those parts back again.

When someone dies, they can no longer tell you who they are. All you have left then is who they were to you. While they were alive, it was a process. Unfolding. Evolving. Once they're gone though, it's all just nostalgia—which in Greek means "homesickness." It's all just uprooted-ness and exile.

Once they are gone, then, I gather, you have to re-evaluate the process itself. Re-evaluate the process-ness of it. Its immediacy—and how immediacy guarantees a future. And how without immediacy there is no future.

At this point, it becomes a practical problem: how do you live in a present with no future? Because someone severed the connection. Cut the cable.

The clues are everywhere, especially in the fact that you just keep getting blown into the future with every breath you take—or is taken in you—whether you like it or not. It's not like you don't keep living.

It's about locating immediacy then, I suppose. In the desert. Achieving conscious contact. Where do you find that door, that window, that secret passageway? How do you close the front door? And we're not even talking here on the level of the marvelous. We're talking the quotidian; we're talking just folks and comfort food. We're talking skin hunger and remembering that a moment of awkwardness is always worth an instant of human warmth. Hugging and being hugged. (Ugh!) We're talking what you choose to nurture and tend, what you feed. And how it is possible to freeze to death without dying.

Come, Holy Spirit, come! Quicken me.

Or better, give me water in my desert sojourn. Give me the courage to take the cool water offered. The manna, the quail. I am so far from home and prone to stupidity and stubbornness. Stiff- necked.

Let me own my thirst. Let me own my hunger.

And I was twirling ever faster. Flames of love. And my feet were not touching the road. Twirling. Twirling. Fucking twirling. Ever faster. Out of control. All elbows and broken limbs. Umbrella carcasses. Flames of love. Out of control. And I was not consumed. Flames of love. Flames of love. I was not consumed.

And the Rabbi said. This is what he said: "See, I told you I'd be here."

And I said. This is what I said: "Uncle."

And he said, "Very funny."

And then he took my hand, and we twirled together, faster and faster. Out of control. And in the heart of the fire. In the fury of the twirl. All elbows and broken limbs. Umbrella carcasses. He held me and gave me shelter. From both himself and myself.

And in a single instant, I knew peace, and, in the space of that single instant, we had breakfast. On the beach. Grilled fish. And it was really good.

While all hell broke loose around us. And something in me died. Just fucking died.

And I was born again. To grieve again. Now and forever. (My baby is gone, gone, gone.) Born again. To fucking grieve again. Now and forever. (My baby is gone, gone, gone.)

In peace.

Ain't I a man now?

Fiery Angels and Hungry Ghosts

The women's menstrual cycles fell into sync. The pomegranates fell heavy and ripe, spilling seeds in the red dust. In the cool stream, large beasts turned over and sighed....

On Ahrens St. in Lombard, Illinois, there were two abandoned houses on our block. One was older and made of brick and was across the street. I could see it from my second-story bedroom window in our split-level ranch. I couldn't have been more than seven. The other was a few houses down on the same side of the street, a subdivision house almost exactly like our own.

One night, the house on the same side of the street caught fire. I awoke to the sound of sirens and lights. I knew that the brick house I could see through my window was not on fire, and I knew that the house just like our own, down the street, was—but the flare from down the street seemed to be reflected on the brick house in such a way that the house itself burned brighter than any real house could. And in the empty attic window of the brick house—a house which had stood for so long, only to be swallowed by a cheap subdivision—and in the empty attic window of the brick house now illuminated by reflected flames, I saw the woman who keens.

I had never imagined such pain and loss. Her hair was wild in the wind from the flames, and her chipped nails slashed at her face like the wings of panicked doves. Her howls pierced the ear. She raised her eyes

and looked at me from across the street and caught my
eye—and it did something to me.

There was a small town somewhere in the south where traveling evangelists and medicine-show professors would winter, waiting for the tent season to come 'round again. After the death of the carnivals and traveling circuses, the whole small town became an unofficial retirement community for all the old carnies and show people—everybody else just moved out—an old folks' home for all the old clairvoyants, for all the old sideshow freaks who were not welcome in their own sideshow freak communities, for reasons just better left alone; for all the old revivalists, for all the old faith healers, spiritualist mediums, purveyors of smut, and whatnot.

The last resident had passed away three years ago at the age of one hundred and one, but the town still continued as if nothing had changed. Lights burned all night in empty houses. Laughter and music could be heard like a great smacking of lips. Spilled whiskey, the smell of blood, and God. Pleasure ran deep until dawn.

Each morning as the sun rose, unblinking cats would appear in the windows of the empty houses and bungalows and stare outward.

At night, when the lights came on in the empty houses and bungalows, the cats would disappear.

When I was in third grade, my mother told me about her sister, Clara, who had died shortly after birth, before my mother was born. Her own mother, our Big Mama, told her once and never talked about her again, although there was a picture that was secured to a shelf in the trailer.

One day, my mother was taking a nap, and I could see that the air around her nose was disturbed, like the air above black tar roads on a hot day. Soon afterward, something grew in my dreams. Over time, it took the form of a baby.

And after a while, in my waking hours, I realized that it was Clara, and that the disturbed air I had seen around my mother's nose was Clara either giving my mother breath or stealing it—like a cat. Of course, it's impossible to know if my seeing the disturbed air was for my own benefit or my mother's. Either way, I've never said anything to her about it.

Still, even as an adult, I sometimes imagine my mother waking up with a start, and seeing in the twilight between wakefulness and sleep those infant eyes staring at her, and being unable to scream. Unable to breathe. Not knowing if she is receiving a gift or being violated. My mother has always said that she never should have had children.

Sometimes when I was younger, angels who had been set on fire waited for me on the outskirts, along the tree lines of pumpkin patches, shifting track signals and changing train schedules, just so that I would see them and, in seeing them, have my destiny changed.

In my youth, I took the angels for granted and let them burn. When their lights extinguished one after the other with a *pop*, I did not mourn or understand the gravity of the situation.

I am older now, and I mourn the angels. I see them against their mad Ray Conniff sky. I repent of my self-absorption and willful blindness.

I was sixteen when I met the woman with windows for eyes. She did not teach me to look far but was an occasion to do so. She was nearly twice my age, in a position of responsibility, and never should have been doing what she was doing with me. It was only later when I realized that the windows of her eyes were two-way mirrors. Sometimes, in the spring, birds would see the reflection of trees in the windows in the front part of our house and break their necks trying to get to them. I have no idea what she saw in the reflection when she looked at me. When I looked at her, I saw far. Through the windows of her eyes. It wasn't until later, when I was a little bit older, when I could see my own reflection. And all the bird carcasses piling up beneath the fractured windows of our eyes.

The air smelling of creosote, I would walk the cross ties until I came to the place where you could find the boxcars, open and idle. I would play there for hours. I would climb in and yell from the open door.

One time, unaware an engine was attached to the boxcar, I heard a screech and felt the boxcar lurch. I was paralyzed. I could not jump. I felt the train pulling out. And me going with it to some other life. And I knew that this other life would be cold. I knew this other life would be dark. I must have jumped because I still have this life.

Still, I am afraid that part of me never did jump and that the train did pull out and take me away and that a part of me really did ride the rails—cold and hungry, just like a ghost—and that that part is going to return someday, very angry, and demand to share the fruits of my life now.

Seems like something in me always wants back in.

There was a small town, and used to be it was a pretty fine place to live. But that was a long time ago. Other small towns were close enough to big cities that they just got absorbed into suburbs and sprawl. This small town was far enough out that it just got forgotten.

The first thing that happened after this town got forgotten was a storm. In the midst of this storm, all the roads in town got picked up and dropped in new places, so that nothing led to where it used to. Nobody could find their relatives. And that made no sense. And so, the people of this town got lonely.

The second thing that happened after the town got forgotten was that the loneliness turned toxic. This happens from time to time. The longing turns inward and, finding no suitable object, turns bitter and sour. What was once gentle now becomes violent. What was once a jest now becomes a judgment.

Which leads to the third thing that happened after the town got forgotten. The citizens lost all sense of proportion, unable to distinguish between a mere slight and a provocation that needed response. They mounted campaigns against their neighbors and found meaning in the purity, the authenticity, of their hatred.

There is a hole in the center of America, and a great sucking that emanates from that hole. We are always in danger of being sucked up into that hole. And emerging on the other side.

There was a tree I knew in Illinois. It had been struck by a tornado and half its roots, ripped from the earth, were laid bare, while some of its branches were driven into the earth like stakes. What was usually hidden was exposed, and what was usually exposed was hidden.

I saw the tree once in New Jersey. I mean, I didn't make a big deal about it. But I saw it.

Lately, it's been coming 'round here in Michigan. It's beautiful. It's really grown into itself.

And yet it is not of this world. Its very presence burns.

This tree is holy.

...with these very hands, I have myself, planted trees. And I have walked with the ladies of the garden. Back and forth, back and forth, along the wall, all night long. Waiting.

Abundantly

"The thief comes only to steal and kill and destroy. I came that they may have life, and have it abundantly."
John 10:10

"Is there anyone among you who, if your child asks for bread, will give a stone?"
Mathew 7:9

I was walking down the Plymouth Road, and it was morning, and it was me and the Rabbi. And we were famished. And we came upon a clearing, and, in the clearing, there were a stone and a loaf of bread.

"You hungry?" the Rabbi asked.

"Always," I said.

"Me too."

"I could eat a horse," I said.

"I could eat a generation," he said.

We looked at the stone and the loaf of bread.

"Which one should we choose?" I asked, a little disappointed.

"Well, the bread would fill the belly, but you're gonna get hungry again..." he started.

"...and the stone would fill the mouth, but the tongue is gonna get tired of tasting it." I finished

We looked at the stone and the bread.

"What if we held out for something better?" I asked.

"More nourishing than stone, tastier than bread?"

"Yeah. That's what I mean."

"Well, we could hold off. But we would suffer."

"Suffer? But wouldn't it be worth it if we could find something better?"

"I don't know Pilgrim, could be in vain. I've seen a lot of people starve. There are more Hunger Artists than you would expect."

"So what do you want to do?" I asked.

"I'm hungry. I want breakfast," he said.

And suddenly before us on the seashore there were a charcoal fire and fish.

The smell was enticing, heavenly.

I was wracked with nausea and vomited.

"You can't accept nourishment, can you?" he asked.

I retched in the sand.

"I knew it! Everything you need is right here," he said, tucking into the fish and then licking his fingers, "and you won't take it."

I watched the Rabbi enjoy his meal. And resented the hell out of him and his pleasure. I heaved in the gutter.

"I...don't...." I stammered.

"Spit it out, Pilgrim!"

"I don't like fish."

"Speak up, you're practically whispering!"

"I don't like *fish, alright*?" I screamed.

"Well, why didn't you say so? We've got chicken, you know."

And suddenly, there were a roast chicken and stuffing and mashed potatoes and gravy. Green beans, onions, and almond slivers. Macaroons.

My stomach rumbled, and my mouth watered.

"Pilgrim?"

"Yeah?" I said, drooling.

"Sometimes, you just have to have the courage to ask for what you want."

"How are you supposed to know what you want?"

"Maybe you could try paying attention."

"This isn't about fish or chicken, is it?"

"Nope"

"It smells good."

"Take. Eat."

I took. I ate.

And the Rabbi ate his fish, and I ate my chicken, our fingers and lips slick with grease.

And when we were finished, our hearts and our bellies were full, and our tongues had no tale to tell, and we were continent, as the waves crashed on the shores of the Plymouth Road. Sweeping out to sea. The poverty. Of the stone and the bread.

Afterword

I started writing *Down the Plymouth Road* sometime in 2011 and finished in early 2018. It was the time after what my wife and I came to call "The Deaths."

In a period of five years, my wife lost her entire family. First her father, then her mother, and then her sister—all to cancer. By the last death, we'd been at my church in New York City for fifteen years, a community we'd loved dearly. And it's not as if I hadn't done my share of funerals. We felt the need to leave. Mary's son, my stepson, was in college. We'd got him through high school. And we'd had enough of death.

Hoping to make a new start, we landed in New Jersey at a church that turned out to be a bad fit. It was outside of Princeton in a culture we could not understand. It didn't go well, and, within two years, we had to move on.

We ended up in Lansing, Michigan. This isn't as random as it might seem. I had gone to high school in the Detroit suburb of Plymouth, outside of Ann Arbor, and Mary's family had a cottage on the shores of Lake Michigan. Every summer, we would drive from the City to the Lake. When the opportunity in Lansing arose, it seemed like a good fit.

And it was. After wandering, we'd found our new home. But we were not done with the Deaths. In the summer of 2017, Mary passed away unexpectedly. She went in for routine surgery, caught an infection, and did not survive.

Because we could not stop for Death, he kindly stopped for us. What are you going to do?

That's what was going on on the outside. *Down the Plymouth Road* was what was going on on the inside. It was written piecemeal in real time, vignette by vignette. When I had enough parts, I stuck them together to form a series. I added each series to the whole, like links to a chain, and then rearranged things, tweaked them, until a rough narrative seemed to emerge. Looking for what remains after the Deaths.

And then kept walking.

Love is relentless.